T0374209

BETRAYAL

ANTONIO F. VIANNA

authorHOUSE®

AuthorHouse™
1663 Liberty Drive
Bloomington, IN 47403
www.authorhouse.com
Phone: 1 (800) 839-8640

© *2017 Antonio F. Vianna. All rights reserved.*

No part of this book may be reproduced, stored in a retrieval system, or transmitted by any means without the written permission of the author.

Published by AuthorHouse   09/14/2017

ISBN: 978-1-5462-0834-1 (sc)
ISBN: 978-1-5462-0833-4 (e)

Library of Congress Control Number: 2017914090

Print information available on the last page.

Any people depicted in stock imagery provided by Thinkstock are models, and such images are being used for illustrative purposes only. Certain stock imagery © Thinkstock.

This book is printed on acid-free paper.

Because of the dynamic nature of the Internet, any web addresses or links contained in this book may have changed since publication and may no longer be valid. The views expressed in this work are solely those of the author and do not necessarily reflect the views of the publisher, and the publisher hereby disclaims any responsibility for them.

PROLOGUE

There are "naturals" everywhere in life, from the athletes to the artists, from the businesspersons to the scientists, as well as from the hustlers who game people by betraying their trust for their own personal gain.

You may have been told never to completely trust anyone, and that definitely meant everyone. Always be prepared to be swindled, ripped-off, scammed, deceived, hoodwinked, tricked, misled, sweet-talked, lured, have a fast one pulled on you, taken in … in other words betrayed … because the devil is closing in from behind, moving fast, and out to get you. And when you think you've discovered that your long time best friend hasn't been genuine with you, you might also realize that the alleged best friend was the real devil who's been moving in on you … or the business proposition that seemed too good to be true wasn't really true at all … or the lover who earnestly said she'd commit to you but conveniently left out the part that the commitment was for only a short time together with you, a one-night transaction.

And when it happens to you … and it will surely happen to you as much as you'll try to deny it … you're not sure how you should feel or what you should do because according to your recollection it's never happened to you before, at least not by anyone you can recollect at the moment, which is one of the most common approaches humankind takes ... self-betrayal is the most common lie we inflict upon ourselves. Maybe you're just at a place in life when you just don't care anymore. You're just too tired and want to forget about it, hide it away in some secret place that you hope you'll forget about, and that no one will find. You're not going to run away because you know the devil is hovering someplace near you, and you can't outrun the devil. You're also not going to fight it out for whatever reason you come up with. It seems that you're just going to give up ... or ... and this is important ... maybe you'll get as mad as hell and do something about it. But then again, maybe you won't.

Lastly ... and this is important so I'm repeating it ... don't overlook self-betrayal ... conning yourself to believe in something that is flatly untrue and that leads you to do something ill-advised.

It's a wonder how anyone makes it through life in a healthy way. But come to think of it, maybe no one does!

CHAPTER 1

It is Friday night as Whitney Danica slowly steps into the bar, seemingly hesitant at first to commit. It's been a few months since she felt the urge to socialize after being dumped by someone she thought she'd have a long and happy life with. Maybe urge isn't the right word … perhaps courage is a better fit.

She takes in a deep breath, lifts her head and looks around, but all she sees are strangers. There's no one she recognizes but why would she … she's been cooped-up for a while that she's almost forgotten who she really is. Then she drifts off into thinking of the past.

It seems so long ago, in a way, in a far distant past that it happened, but the truth is it happened recently. Whitney's memory now, to a certain extent, a bit thinned by passing time in spite of it being just a short time ago, and also, she suspects, wanting to wipe it entirely clean and dirt-free from her memory. Yet for some reason she can't or conceivably doesn't want that to happen. The truth may be she really doesn't know. And, yes, there are possibly other reasons that are too painful to remember as well, so she thinks.

She never considered she was being set-up for a hard and painful fall of disappointment. Was it her fault through ignorance that she didn't pick up on the clues, or was it so well camouflaged that there would be no way she'd know what was happening?

Whitney wonders if anyone really cares what happened to her then and how it affects her now, emotionally, physically, and spiritually? In other words, what does it matter and who really cares one way or another? But she is now, soaking wet with the feelings, soaked to the skin and wet through, almost like a drowned rat, trying to squeeze out the memories. Cathartic to remember and tell, sure, but personally, to be honest, she thinks it all seems so pathetic … just ask her. Whitney thinks her caution in all of this has something to do with some strongly held belief or beliefs about something or another: shut-up, and deal with it head on. Don't hide or run away from it … fight it head on. Or, perhaps this has been on her bucket list for a while and now it's risen to the top through elimination of all the other items so that there's nothing else on the list. But even that sounds crazy, silly, ridiculous and idiotic to her. And come to think of it, Whitney notices how many words she's already used to persuade herself against discussing "IT."

Is she really trying to set aside for now, or perhaps forever, getting on with the topic? What's really going on?

Whitney is now surprised by how quickly they fell into the same habits that was suggestive of a contented couple … they didn't want to be apart even if each of them was doing something quite different from each other.

It seemed they had everything they had always wanted in a relationship. It seemed so easy, perhaps too easy and unreal. She never once wondered if it would survive time and never … definitely never … did she think that the devil was fast closing in.

"Hi." A man about her age smiles at her as he walks to be by her side. "I'm Jimmy." He extends his hand.

She looks at him without actually seeing him. She used to be able to profile men very well, but now she feels the accumulation of rust. Whitney reminds herself that it's all about practice. Then she snaps out of the self-imposed trance to quickly notice his extended hand, slightly nods approval of his good looks, and smiles. "Good to meet you. I'm Whitney." She takes his hand in hers, squeezes it just a little and then releases her grip. Her skill set is returning more quickly than she thought it would. She begins to feel more like her former self, and it feels good … very good.

He feels his heart rate pick up a wee bit. "Please to meet you."

She asks, "Seems as if there's a party going on here with everyone knowing one another here. Do you know them?"

He nods no, and then shrugs his shoulders, "Came with a few buddies. One of them knows who's throwing the party. And you?"

"I don't recognize anyone." She puckers her rich red looking lips. She's feeling her mojo return. "You look like the actor. Oh, who is he? Damn, I can't remember his name or the name of the movie. Sorry." She shakes her head sideways and dips her head ever so slightly to suggest embarrassment, but only she knows she's faking it. She's definitely getting back into her former groove before "IT" happened.

"Nope, I'm not him … whoever he is." His eyes widen thinking she just gave him a compliment. "Have you acted or maybe you're an actress?"

"What do you think?" Her parted mouth shows off her white and even teeth.

"If you're not, you should."

"What does that mean?"

He hesitates, suddenly stumped himself as to what he meant. "Well, let's talk about something else." He raises his eyebrows.

"For example?" She steps closer to him, now within a few inches of each other. She feels in total control, just as it used to be. And the feeling is sensational to her.

He shrugs his shoulders, and blurts out the first thing that comes to his mind. "You sure are beautiful." His face turns red.

"And what was that supposed to mean?" Her face is no longer cheerful, but quite serious looking.

"I – I didn't mean that. Sorry." He backs away one step. He's definitely surprised by her action.

"Oh, I know what you meant and so do you." She takes a full step toward him to keep the same distance as before. "You want to go to bed with me. You're like all the rest of them."

"Please, please, I'm sorry, no, I didn't mean that at all."

"What exactly did you mean?"

"I – I …." His voice trails off.

"Let me be perfectly honest with you." She pauses. Her eyes are targeted and aligned directly with his. A slight cocky smile plays out on her face. "Beds really don't interest me all that much, they never have. I prefer other ways."

A short time later Jimmy flicks the light on and kicks

the door shut of his apartment. Whitney and he are instantly into each other's arms in a hot-blooded embrace. Before he can shift his position, she quickly removes her shoes, undoes her blouse and gets out of her slacks. She stands in her bikini panties. Then she goes for his clothes ... removing everything he's wearing without any resistance from him.

"The bedroom is over here." Jimmy isn't able to keep up with her speed of undressing.

"I've already said beds don't interest me." Nearly naked, she parades toward him, hips slowly swaying in a hypnotic rhythm.

By now, being totally stripped down, he feels tension build between his legs.

She drops her eyes to look at his erection, smiles, and quickly jumps to straddle him in a perfect position.

Their two craving bodies slide down onto the carpeted floor, thirsting for unbridled sex without any thought of foreplay. They grope, grasp, gasp and fondle each other in a fever of sexual hunger. She mounts him, crying out with increasing jubilance. She then screams, followed by a long sigh, as he loses all control over his own bodily function. When it comes to an end they close their eyes in each other's embrace until the chill of the next morning wakes them up.

It is 5:00 am the next morning, Saturday. Whitney is up before him.

He turns over once and then reverses his position, hand swaying to find her naked body. Obviously, he doesn't. He opens his eyes to notice at once a blanket covering him. Confused by the existence of the cover and absence of

Whitney next to him he shifts his eyes to see her standing alongside a dim lit lamp. He is in full endorsement of her appearance, so he stays quiet as he continues to admire her beautiful buck naked body.

She leans forward to flick the ash of her cigarette into an empty cup that she found in the kitchen. She takes one final drag from the cigarette and then stuffs it completely out in the same cup. Her nakedness and the curves of her body remain in full view for Jimmy to admire.

Her senses have now returned to a finely tuned instrument. With her back to him she says, "You seemed a little cold last night so I found the blanket on your bed." Her voice is soft and scrumptious sounding to his ears.

He stays quiet while he continues to soak it all in. He hopes … really hopes … it's not another one of his erotic dreams.

She continues, "Last night was good for me. I didn't realize how much I needed it. Thanks." She turns to face him with nipples perfectly situated on her sweet looking breasts. "How about you?"

He takes in a deep swallow, astonished at how he is lost for words. He's never met anyone like her before. All he can do is to nod his head a few times. Then he coughs and takes in another gulp of needed air. He concludes this is the real thing, not a dream.

"I was married for less than a year … something like that. I don't really want to remember. I thought I was happy. Maybe I just pretended to be happy, at least that's what the analyst said, to pretend to be happy and sane." She laughs in a guttural sound. She's not interested if he's listening or interested in her story. That's not the point. It's all about how she feels.

"My husband ran off with his boyfriend. Can you believe that? I had no idea he was gay, none what-so-ever, honestly." She shakes her head a few times.

"And so I had an affair with my analyst. Why not, I needed someone at that moment and it was costing me a ton of money for the sessions, so I figured I'd get the most out of the fee." She flickers her eyebrows, extends her arms forward and close to her sides with the palms up.

"He told me I was a lame lay. I had no idea that I was so bad. Maybe that's what drove my former husband to change teams." She lets out another guttural laugh, tilts her head downward and slightly shakes it sideways a few times.

Then she reaches for another cigarette and lights it up. While taking in a deep drag, she looks up towards the ceiling. "I apparently have a masculine disposition. I get aroused quickly, I climax prematurely, and I can't wait to get my clothes back on to leave. I seem to be inept at intimacy issues but I'm goddam good at my work."

She takes another long drag of the cigarette and blows the smoke into the open air. "Don't take this the wrong way. I enjoyed last night, but it's time for me to go. Don't try to get in touch with me. I'm not interested. I'm not much for commitments these days, except for work, so I'll betray you the first chance I get."

Before she finishes the last few drags of the cigarette, he sits up. The blanket is still covering his lower body. "When I was a kid, my best buddies edged me to fist fight a really big kid from another neighborhood to prove to them we were tougher than them. I didn't want to fight … anyone … at any time ... but I was edged on because I was the biggest kid on the block."

She sits down, legs crossed, still totally naked with the cigarette still between her fingers. She nods as if to grant him permission to continue, although she's quite not interested in hearing him go on but she figures she's got to finish the cigarette before she leaves.

He stares at her crotch, swallows deeply and then continues. "Anyway, against my will, I betrayed myself and fought the big kid because I didn't want to offend my buddies ... I wanted them to still like me. I was, in fact, their role model of some sort and I couldn't disappoint them in spite of going against my personal values. So, I fought the best I could, but got a shellacking from the big kid. He was faster and stronger than I had anticipated."

"Shit happens." She takes another drag from the cigarette. Her face is neutral looking as if she is unmoved by the story. Her eyes are glued to his.

"After my pathetic performance, I laid on the ground as my buddies just stared at me in surprise at the outcome. No one said a word, even for the big kid who simply turned and walked away. I saw the disbelief in their eyes ... shocked and rendered speechless. Aside from my bruised body, I didn't like myself for going against my moral compass, so I slowly got to my feet and started to walk away. My buddies followed me, telling me I did the best I could do, but now was the time to forget about it. It was over. But it wasn't over for me. In fact, it really all started for me. I didn't like what I did. I fought in spite of personally opposing to do it. I, in fact, betrayed myself because I didn't want to disappoint my buddies." His eyes are now swelled with tears. He sniffles and then he rubs his nose with the back of his hand.

"Yeah, crappy story, but not something that rocks my socks off. You don't see me crying over it."

He frowns. "You're hardened. Doesn't anything bother you?"

"Yeah, what's with the pistachios in the kitchen?"

He frowns, confused by the question, "the pistachios?"

"Yeah, what's with them? Peanuts or cashews, maybe, but pistachios, I don't understand."

He clears his throat, still not sure of the relevance of her statement, but he answers just the same. "They fuel my fitness."

Her laugh is much more than an expression of amusement. She almost doubles up in hysterics.

He isn't entertained by her response. His voice is now a bit harsh and louder. "What's your problem?"

"My problem? I don't have a problem. It's you … you've been conned by the advertiser … bamboozled! Don't you get it? It's as clear as day. And you better wake up before it's too late."

He is lost for words, so he keeps quiet, yet inside he feels his stomach churn with anger.

"And the POM shit in the refrigerator. What's that for? Haven't you heard of white wine … you know, like Chardonnay? Where's the coffee, orange juice, and bagels?" She waits for a response but when there isn't one, she continues. There is an obvious smirk on her face. "Oh, sorry, they don't fuel your fitness." She taps her forehead with the palm of her hand, the hand not holding the almost finished cigarette.

She moves towards her clothes that are still on the floor and dresses with a sense of time pressure to get out of the situation. The last remains of the cigarette remain between her lips.

Now at the door, she turns to dip into her pocket to pull out a twenty dollar bill. She places the money on a small table nearby and takes the stub of the finished cigarette out of her mouth to lie alongside the money. "Here, take it and buy some real food." She leaves him alone, silent with his confused thoughts.

Whitney returns to her apartment to change clothes and freshen up. It is now 6:15 am, Saturday. The recent affair with Jimmy is now completely out of her mind. No sense to remember insignificant people, places or things. It only clouds your thinking and takes up precious space in your brain.

Before leaving her apartment she finishes drinking her third cup of coffee, and finally gives one last look of her appearance in the mirror. "Exceptional," she says to the reflection as she approvingly nods.

She takes a cab to head off for work, something she's done without a break for as long as she can remember. Working on Saturdays, and an occasional Sunday or Holiday, keeps her in front of her peer group and fully noticed by the Executives. She figures today is no exception. However, she will be surprised, and she definitely doesn't like surprises unless she starts them.

Perhaps it's due to her refined senses or maybe something else, but Whitney senses something different as she steps out of the cab in front of the Corporate Office. She confidently walks towards the revolving doors and once inside the building she suddenly stops.

The security guards are not the same personnel as from just yesterday and their uniforms are different as well … color and style. There is a metal detector and tunnel-like apparatus that people walk through as a uniformed guard with a clipboard writes something on a piece of paper. A photographer is stationed at the end of the inspection process taking a photo of each and every one who enters.

"Hey, what going on?" Her loud voice and slow pace towards one of the guards get his attention.

"Stop there! Do not move any further." A guard approaches Whitney. "Who are you and what is the nature of your business?" He holds a clipboard and ballpoint pen. His eyes are steely serious looking.

"I work here! What's it to you?" She mirrors the guard's unyielding stare.

"I'll repeat my two questions. Who are you and what is the nature of your business?"

"I presume you are hard of hearing, so get it checked. I'm Whitney Danica, I work here as a Senior Manager. Here is my I.D. card." She pulls out of her pocket the Company's photo I.D. card to hand over to the guard.

The guard reaches for the item, takes a quick look before answering. He nods his head. "I understand the confusion Ms. Danica. The Company has been sold and the process has changed. I'll call H. R.. Please wait over there." He points to two empty chairs.

"Sold? Why wasn't I told of this?" Her widen opened eyes show her surprise and anger. "I'm a Senior Manager! I should have been advised of this!"

"Please take a seat. I'm sure the head of H. R., Mr. Samuelson, will clarify everything. Please, just take a seat."

"Samuelson? Do you mean Sheldon Samuelson? Is that who you're referring to?"

"Yes Ms. Danica, he is the one." His firm answer adequately hides his increased annoyance of her.

"He was a low level supervisor or something else insignificant in customer service. What's he now doing as the chief H. R. person?"

"I'll let him explain. Please, Ms. Danica, have a seat. I'm sure it will be a short wait for him." He repeats pointing to the spot of the two empty chairs.

"I want my I.D. returned to me!" She puts out her open hand.

"I'm sure Mr. Samuelson will explain everything. Please, take a seat." He nods his head toward the two empty chairs. He'd like to give her a good punch but knows better. Somebody could easily be videoing it all and then place it on the Internet. It would probably go viral.

"Somebody has an awful lot of explaining to me." Her voice is a wee-bit lower as she stomps towards the empty chairs. She flops down and crosses her arms. "This is all crap." She shakes her head in disgust. Then her voice is loud. "I should have been told of this!"

People near and far hear her shout, yet no one steps forward to do anything about it but they all silently agree with her.

Fifteen minutes pass without Samuelson's appearance. Whitney is about to make a fuss about the situation. She stands, preparing for the outburst, when she recognizes Samuelson walking her way. Her body is fully erect. "It's about time! What's going on here?"

Samuelson is short and pudgy, fat hanging over his belt in spite of his suit coat buttoned to hide his tubby appearance. He waddles towards her with a phony smile that fools no one. "Hello Whitney." He extends his hand for a fake friendly handshake.

She raises her right hand to point her finger directly at him. "What the hell is going on?"

He puts aside for the time being her display of defiance. "Don't get so worked up. There's been a buyout with new owners. Some employees will be displaced, some already have. Come with me so I can fill you in." He nods for her to follow him to his office.

"Who are they? I want to know who the new owners are!"

"Later, there's gonna be an announcement that will clarify it all," he lies not knowing himself the answer.

She walks step for step alongside him. "What did you do to get your job?" Her face is full of displeasure, creases in her forehead and lips clenched tightly. "Whose ass did you kiss?"

He ignores her comments as he continues walking, doing his best to keep his cool and not share his most inner thoughts about how he feels about her. They walk up two flights of stairs taking the stairwell to a small office. He steps in first to get behind a worn out gray metal desk in order to stay in control of the situation. As he sits down in the accompanying metal chair he forces another smile and then points to two metal chairs in front of the desk. "Please, close the door and take a seat."

"I want it kept open." Her defiance continues as she sits in one of the two metal chairs.

They sit across from each other like passengers on a train, heads tilting towards the worn train car floor, not yet willing to speak, only anxious to get off at the next stop.

He ignores her comment but doesn't move. The door remains open.

She doesn't look him in the eyes, but rather focuses her attention to his chin, not wanting yet to see what lives behind them. She feels as if a cube of ice is slowly sliding down her spine, and all sounds are suddenly cut off to an eerie silence, not even hearing herself think. She then turns her look to see his eyes stare her way as if he is a cobra with his hood fully exposed, ready to strike. She wonders if this is the short beginning for a quick end to her career. Has she suddenly become the proverbial canary in the coal mine?

His voice is calm and soft. "As I said a few minutes ago, there's been a buyout with new owners. Some employees will be displaced, some already have." He's said the words so many times already to himself that he's memorized the words exactly without much emotion or care one way or another. "Notices have gone out to all the employees. Some will have to reapply for their jobs, some others will not. A few will be assigned to other positions from their previous ones. Should anyone of these employees refuse the new assignment, they'll be given a severance package according to our current policies and in compliance with all Federal and State laws. You're in this category. Do you want to know the new job?"

When you're at the top of your game, it's easy to forget how difficult it was to get there ... the long hours, hard work, minimal family gatherings, friends dismissed, and healthy habits discarded. But it's real easy to betray yourself that it will all continue indefinitely ... until one day it happens ... fast and without warning ... you fail and don't have the strength to get up ... you stop believing in yourself, your passion, and your enthusiasm. You see your foreseeable future ending. But too often people don't see the handwriting on the wall and therefore can't adjust as the wall comes crashing down.

Her tongue slowly licks her lips. She takes in a deep breath and asks, "What's the new job?"

"You'll still be a Senior Manager without any pay grade adjustment. Same total compensation package as before, just doing something different." He inhales and slowly lets out the air, enjoying the suspense he's created with a person he's never liked or respected. He stares at her without blinking, uttering another word, or any body movement as he wonders if she has somehow read his thoughts.

She asks him a question in a calm and controlled voice hoping she doesn't know the answer. "What is the something different?"

Their eyes lock as if each knows what the other is thinking. Then he blinks once. "You'll be moving from promoting Gracie's Biscuits to the foreign market to Debbie's Donuts to the domestic market."

She is frozen with a silent scream of shock, eyes remained fixated on him. "That's going from a cash cow to a dog. I'm running a business that exhibits a return on assets that is greater than the market growth rate, and thus generates more cash than it consumes. And now you're going to give me a dog with low market share and a low growth rate and thus neither generating nor consuming a large amount of cash. Dogs are cash traps because of the money tied up in a business that has little potential. Such businesses are candidates for divestiture. Is that what you ultimately want to do with me … divest me from the Company by giving me a dog? Is that the ulterior motive?"

"I don't make the decisions, I'm just executing them."

"You don't even know what I'm talking about! You have no business sense what-so-ever!"

"Take it or leave it. That's how it is."

"I need time to think this over." She gets quiet all of a sudden for a short time, something that is very comfortable for him. Then she lights up. "Who's on my staff … who's working for me? I want the same people … no changes … I know them and how they work and they know me. This is not negotiable!"

"I'll see what I can do."

"No, it's what it will be, or didn't you hear me about it not being negotiable!"

He has a bit of a temper, but usually it is well controlled as in this time … he sits on his rage. He'd really like to smack her in the face. "I'll see what I can do." He swallows. "Is that it?"

"You've got until Monday morning. I typically arrive no later than seven in the morning." She stares directly into his eyes. "Oh, I almost forgot … same office or something different?"

"That's easy to answer … same office, same floor."

He looks at his wristwatch before fixating his stare at her

to signal the meeting has ended. "Oh, one more thing ... you'll be signing new paperwork on Monday."

"I'm not finished, so stop looking at your Mickey Mouse watch. I want to meet the new owners. Who are they and what are their strategic business plans for this outfit? I want to know my future with them!"

"Whitney, in due time, be patient."

"Patience is tolerance of time wasted."

He watches her with an unblinking stare as does a wolf drinking from water's edge. He waits for her to do something unexpected. He is not surprised.

As she stands to turn around and allegedly walk out, she hesitates as she tucks her hair behind her ear. She twirls around as if she is a spinning top, moves her head in just the right way to get a good look at him. She giggles, but not in the way of being embarrassed or nervous. She giggles, as in a snicker, an evil snicker to be more precise. "I've changed my mind."

His surprise look is not the kind of expression as if he had just won the lottery without buying a ticket. It's a surprise look of fear. He is scared that something is about to happen that he won't be able to defend against, akin to a nightmare that won't go away because you can't wake up.

Her facial expression is as distinctly unfriendly as the words she uses and the tone of her voice. "I want to meet the new owners today, a one-on-one with them, to understand what's really going on and my role in all of this."

He clears his throat, about to repeat what he had previously said, but he is quickly cut off.

"Shh." She puts her right index finger to her mouth, and then begins an untruth realizing everyone has secrets they want kept hidden. "I know who you really are … your past and what you've done. You're not proud of it but prefer to keep everything hush-hush. I know … I really do. I'll keep private what I know about you and you'll make sure the meeting happens, a simple something for something … a quid pro quo."

His empty voice matches his slackened face, now believing the ugly truth that she knows something about him that he prefers kept buried forever. He wonders how she knows, and what else she might be aware of, giving no thought that perhaps she's just bluffing.

"I'm sure they're in the building someplace, and that you know their extension. Make the call now … indicate it's important to meet with me within the hour. I'll handle the rest."

He very much wants to grab her by the throat and squeeze as tightly as he can, but he obviously knows better. He'd have to dispose of the body someway and for the moment can't think how! He clears his throat and forces a smile that is insincere to both of them. "Hold your horses. Step outside the office, and take a seat while I make a call."

Whitney is still standing and slightly leaning forward to emphasize her point. "Make it snappy." She turns to leave him alone.

Now outside Samuelson's office she waits in a small and cluttered waiting area. The furniture seems to be direct cousins of what he has in his office. She smirks, shakes her head sideways all the time expecting to be with the executive group shortly. Yet her mind drifts to an unpleasant time she'd care to forget but for some reason can't. It happened at an important time in her career. She remembers exactly what happened and how she felt. She was at an important meeting, ready to say what was on her mind … it was essentially her best pitch ever conceived, or so she thought … and was convinced she'd have their full and positive attention … and then came the unexpected incident. At first everyone seemed to listen without saying a word, something she interpreted as positive. Some even gave a slight nod of the head that she interpreted as positive, but mostly they were quiet. And then came the unexpected incident, faster than she could have ever imagined … one person turned against her followed by others who joined in until that's all there was to hear … at times it even turned hostile and got very personal by bringing up things that happened so long ago and she thought had been forgotten. It was at that point in time that she felt betrayed.

"I'm sorry to bother you now, but you said to call if something important was happening."

The Chief Legal Counsel's voice is calm yet annoyed by the unexpected call from Samuelson. "What is it?"

"It's Whitney Danica. She's demanding to have a meeting with Mr. Charles Whitehead, you and the President about her career."

"So she knows?"

"Yes, she was coming to work today when the new security team stopped her. They called me and she unloaded. The notices have been sent out to all employees and should arrive in their mail today, but she arrived at work this morning before her mail."

"She works on Saturdays?"

"It seems that's all she does is work, sometimes even on Sundays and Holidays."

"That dedicated, huh?"

"I'd say that neurotic and compulsive."

"I remember reading her personnel file. She's someone we want to keep if I recall."

"Yet the new assignment she's been given seems to be a demotion, at least that's what she thinks."

"So you told her before she received the letter."

"Yes, maybe I shouldn't have, but she was headed towards her office and would have figured it out quickly enough."

"Stay on the line while I talk this over with Mr. Whitehead."

"Yes sir." As Samuelson waits he hears sounds of a conversation through the phone that is too blurred and indistinguishable to make out. He figures the men are talking it through.

Ten minutes later he hears the Chief Legal Counsel's voice again. This time it sounds more relaxed. "Send her up." The phones disconnect.

Minutes later Whitney meets the new Chief Executive in his office on the top floor of the building. Joining him are the Chief Legal Counsel and the President.

"Thank you for squeezing in a few minutes within your

busy schedule to meet me. I'm very appreciative." She feels the spirit of the adventure.

Mr. Hank Rose, the Chief Legal Counsel, cocks his head to the side as stoniness comes into his eyes knowing she's up to no good. He is the first to speak. "Mr. Samuelson indicated you had something quite urgent to share with Mr. Whitehead." He is 56 years old, is clean shaven, short cut black hair, white shirt, and pinstriped suit with black shoes and matching socks, all by Vuitton.

Mr. Charles Whitehead, the Chief Executive Officer, is 56 years old with a razor thin mustache and no other noticeable facial hair. He has a full head of curly brown hair. He is dressed in a blue linen sport coat, black turtleneck, black pants with black shoes and matching socks, all designed by Tessuto's of Italy.

Mr. Fred Saunders, the son-in-law of Charles, the President, is 31 years old, without facial hair but with a full head of black hair combed straight back. He wears an opened black colored shirt, black pants, and shoes without socks, from the Zegna collection.

"Yes, that's correct. It's about the business and what Mr. Samuelson told me about the restructuring. I've been here for seven years, approaching that milestone in a month. I know firsthand our product lines, what customer needs will be satisfied, and how our products and services are unique to the customer. I know our customers, who they are, what their profiles are, where they live, work and play, their buying habits, and their needs. I know our competition, who they are and where they're located, their strengths and weakness, and how might they respond to our products and services. I know our suppliers, who they are, where they're located, their business practices, and what relationships can be expected from them. I know our physical facilities and our equipment. I know the legal and regulatory environment. I know how cultural, social and international environments influence our industry and our specific business. I know more about people than Samuelson will ever know about people, the availability, the training, the incentives, and what motivates them." She looks deeply into each of the men's eyes and feels thrilled that she has engaged all three of them. She stays silent for a short time, waiting for one of them to say something, to confirm to herself that they're thinking the same way.

Charles Whitehead mumbles, speaks in a rote manner, but the intent look on his face says something quite differently. "Impressive. I like what I hear."

She knows the three men have been profiling her and she likes the outcome. "Thank you. What would be our logical next step?" Her smile is genuine. She keeps her response to as short as possible. No sense in spoiling the meeting, but she does have eyes for the President, a good looking man to her.

Hank Rose and Fred Saunders look at Charles Whitehead patiently waiting for a signal from him. These three men are bound by the secrets they share.

Whitney wonders when they'll get to the point of making a decision. She scans their faces looking for a clue as to what they might be thinking, and even more importantly what they will do next. She thinks she sees a hesitant smirk of satisfaction from Saunders, but that might be based on what she wants to see. Then she clearly sees a slight nod by Whitehead followed by the sound of his voice, a deep and solemn tone.

Then Whitehead says, "This is an important, very important decision we must make. Too much rests on it. And so, I hope you will respect that we need some time together, the three of us, to hash it out." His eyes study her.

She replies with a slow nod, yes, as she studies him. Whitney waits for more to come but when it doesn't happen she figures it's time to leave the three men alone. She glances at each man individually while settling on Charles Whitehead. She decides now isn't the time to ask about who they really are and the nature of the buyout.

Charles Whitehead says, "We might be able to make something happen. We need a few days to think this through. I can't imagine it taking us more time."

Out of the corner of her eye she's convinced she sees Rose give a sympathetic nod while Fred Saunders remains unmoved. "Of course, as much time as necessary. I too think we can make it happen if we all try." She stands, trades looks with each of the men, more of quick glances without anyone responding further. She leaves the three men alone to walk to her office.

Charles is the first to comment. "She just might be the one to take charge of Operation Inquiry." He gives each of the two men a stare waiting for their point of view.

Fred responds first. "I wouldn't trust her one bit. She'd sink her teeth into you at the first chance. No, I wouldn't do it."

Charles turns his head towards Hank, "And you, what do you say about this?"

"If it ever gets out that we're eavesdropping on each and

every one of the employees, we'll have the Feds all over us. I mean, it's one thing of whether companies in general are justified in collecting data that is public knowledge, such as on social media platforms, but it's something else to collect information without their knowing."

Charles snaps back, "So we have to be more innovative in how we do this."

Fred asks, "Like what?"

Charles nods towards Hank to answer. "Almost any device that uses the Internet can collect information. Hell, companies track your Internet queries to post advertisements where you'll see them, to persuade you to buy something. As profit margins get smaller you really can't blame companies to trying to survive any way they can."

Fred says, "And we'll see more litigation."

Hank looks surprised. "Don't play innocent here. You've known all along what's been happening. You voted 'yes' on it, and if my memory serves me right, you were quite enthusiastic about the whole damn project." He continues to stare at Fred. "And further, if I'm not mistaken, you wanted to give each employee a Company gift with the logo such as a mug or something they would put on their desk that had an audio and visual device to listen and watch their every move." He pauses, "Am I right?"

Fred shrugs his shoulders as if getting tangled in his own shorts means nothing.

Charles raises his hand, "OK, boys, let's stop arguing. I agree she's not the one for this." He looks at both men, "But we're still moving ahead with artificial intelligence as it relates to hiring, promotion, and employee loyalty, aren't we?"

Hank picks up. "I'm still looking into available A.I. software that will pick up words printed on a resume, words spoken during an interview, and facial expressions that will tell us someone's temperament on whatever the topic is, such as why he left his former company, what she thought of her boss, whether she would be loyal to our mission, what's his political point of view, and so forth. A few companies are leading the pack in developing algorithms but nobody is close enough to making it worth our while. Maybe in ten years at best case scenario, in my opinion."

Charles noisily lets out a breath of air through his mouth. "OK, back to her." He gives both men a nod. "It seems we're saying 'no' to bring her into Operation Inquiry, but what about something else?"

CHAPTER 2

It's said that for many workers, Monday is the gloomiest day of the week. Employees can't bear the thought of having to spend precious time with a company they don't respect, doing a job they can't stand, and getting paid barely at a living wage. Others also say that it's the unhealthiest day of the week as well, with the highest absenteeism rate … employees calling in sick with sudden illnesses or just feeling down-in-the-dumps the entire time. Maybe it's all psychological or maybe there's more to it than that.

On this particular Monday at this particular Company, the event that is about to happen exceeds the employees' most depressing expectations. It all starts as each employee entering the main lobby of the Corporate Office noticing different security guards outfitted in different uniforms from last week, something that by itself might be unusual, but when each employee is handed an envelope that is personalized to each one, their low-sprits begin.

"What is this?" Janet, a mid-level manager looks at the envelope with her full name printed on it. She stops in her tracks, opens it and then reads. Only her lips move. Then she says aloud, "What?" She looks around at other employees, who mirror her actions.

Richard, an individual contributor without supervisory or managerial responsibility stands only a few feet away from Janet. He frowns, confused as to the meaning. He looks at Janet, "What does yours say?"

"That there's been a Company-reorganization, and I have to report to the main conference room for an important meeting at 9. And yours, what does it say?"

"Same thing about the reorg but not to worry, and that more information will come through the mail within a few days. So just go to my workstation to work."

Janet yells out so everyone in the lobby can hear. "Hey, who got the memo to report to the main conference room at 9?" She notices peer level managers raise their hands. "And who got the one telling you to simply go to your workstation?" She notices hands rise from the non-supervisory employees. She now believes heads will be rolling soon.

While most of the employees go to their workstations, the supervisors and mid-level managers cram into the main conference room. A buzz of overlapping conversations fills the air, no one really hearing the other while each wonders what's going on. More than just a few sense the guillotine of a job loss approaching fast.

Samuelson walks into the conference room. Fat hangs over his belt in spite of his suit coat buttoned to hide his flabby appearance. There is a food stain very near the collar of his shirt that he tried hand rubbing off but that only deepened the spot. He waddles towards the front of the room where there is a podium. He holds onto a few pieces of paper that he'll read from and other pieces with several probable questions with answers. He feels his stomach churn.

He clears his throat. "Ga – good morn – morning." His phony smile fools no one. "I'm Sheldon Samuelson. Some of you may know me from Cu – Customer Service." He blinks a few times, feeling anxious and wishing there was someone else who would do this. "I – I'm now the Director of Human Resources."

Quickly and without warning there is a loud uptick from the employees. While not previously synchronized or practiced in any way, the surprise noise is piercing and unanimous.

Someone from the back of the room yells, "What happened to Doreen?"

Samuelson clears his throat, and then in what can best be described as a whispered tone he says, "She's no longer with the Company."

The same voice asks, "What happened?"

"I'm not at liberty to say." Samuelson definitely wants this meeting to end very fast.

Another employee shouts, "And what did you do to get the job?"

"I – I really don't know. They just asked me." He feels thumping of his heart.

A third employee hollers, "What's going on? Why are we all here?"

A thick layer of murmur continues.

"Well, that's why I'm here." He pulls out a piece of paper to read from. "The Company has been bought by WRS. This means we have new owners. Each employee has been sent via the U.S. mail a personalized letter that explains the purchase. Also, each employee is told in the personalized letter one of three job possibilities. You should have received your letter by now." He sees blank stares from the audience. "I guess not, huh." He swallows, growing nervous each second he's in front of the employees.

Someone yells, "Who are they ... WRS?"

Samuelson's mind goes blank. He's not sure himself but manages to say, "In due time they'll clarify everything."

He is interrupted by another but stronger coat of concerned employee voices shouting out, but he doesn't understand a word they say.

His eyes return to the monologue printed on the paper that now has become dampened from the sweat of his hands. "One job possibility is that your most recent job has been replaced by two different jobs. This means the most recent job no longer exits. In place of it are two new jobs. There are job descriptions and job requirements for each of the two jobs along with a salary range for each new job. The new salary ranges may or may not be the same as the old job. If you're interested in any of the two new jobs you'll have to apply and interview for them."

Another interruption is yelled, "And what if I don't like either of the two jobs? What next?"

Samuelson turns to another piece of paper with questions and answers. He quickly finds the right answer. "Then you'll be given a severance package equal to 1 full week for each full year of employment along with your C.O.B.R.A. benefits."

The same person yells again, "So the thirteen years I've worked here suddenly means nothing! Is that it?"

Samuelson thinks he can adlib the answer, but falls

short in convincing anyone, "I'd say that's pretty healthy. Come on, thirteen weeks of pay."

Suddenly the entire room is silent, not even a whisper of breathing is heard. And then it erupts with shouts of anger, shock, betrayal, and helplessness. The noise is so loud and the anger so intense that the words falling out of their mouths are incoherent.

Samuelson thought he'd had gotten his style down to a pat, but he's obviously mistaken. His body shakes, lips start to tremble, and the only thing he thinks of is getting out of the room as quickly as possible. But without warning the room settles down. He tries to look directly at them but all he sees is a blur. Yet, somehow he feels the paper still in his hand. He looks down towards it and finds the place where he left off. He doesn't remember what the next words are. If he had, he might not have said it. His voice is shaky, "Others of you might receive a notice that your job has been totally eliminated. In that case, you'll get the severance package as I've just described." Once he realizes what he's said, he feels his throat constrict and instinctively thinks of ducking in case something is thrown at him, but that doesn't happen. The audience is stunned. He quickly makes a decision to get to the final scenario as fast as possible. He reads it slowly since this option is neutral. "The third possibility is that there is no change to your job status. In other words, you keep your job, benefits, and salary. Nothing changes." When he looks up to everyone he sees zombie-looking faces. He gulps a breath of air, "Any questions?"

The zombie-status changes as one employee sitting in the front row raises her hand to ask, "When do we meet the new owners?"

Samuelson breaths a little more comfortably knowing the answer, yet to be sure he turns to the question and answer piece of paper. "WRS is planning a celebration party within the next few weeks. I'll keep you posted." He thinks the meeting is over, but it isn't.

A hand lurches upward from someone in the center of the room. She stands. "I haven't received the letter yet but I've applied for a mortgage on a condo. What should I do?"

Samuelson's mind goes blank. He isn't prepared for the question and wonders if he should give her personal advice or leave it alone. "I – I don't know what to say."

Another employee yells from the back, "Don't go through with it. Wait to see what your letter says."

Standing a few feet away someone says, "I've got a kid in college, and we've just been told that tuition is going up. What the hell am I supposed to do?" His voice is desperate sounding.

The same employee from the back provides his advice, "Get a second job. That's what I'm going to do while I look for something else in order to get out of this place."

Murmurs re-emerge.

Samuelson asks, hoping for the last time, "Any other questions?" He looks around, sees no hands raised and is about to adjourn when another employee in the back of the room asks something else.

"I'm pregnant and am going on maternity leave. Will I have my job?"

Someone sitting next to the woman turns towards her and extends a hand on her arm, "You're protected when you're on maternity leave."

"But I'm not on leave yet! It doesn't start for another two weeks!" Her voice is full of hopelessness.

The same guy in the back of the room screams, "You're screwed."

"Will WRS give me a letter of recommendation?"

Murmurs continue.

Samuelson checks with the question and answer sheet. He reads, "WRS will only confirm your dates of employment and job title."

The same employee asks, "Is that it?"

Samuelson makes his statement concise, "Yes."

Another employee who up to this point has been silent asks, "What if I want a copy of my personnel file, will WRS give me it?"

Samuelson looks up the answer, "Yes, that's correct. You'll need to provide a written request to WRS and then within 30 days we'll turn over to you the contents of your personnel file. There will be a charge of 5 cents per page."

Within the murmurs there is the same ire. "Cheap bastards."

"Anything else?" Samuelson hopes this is the end. He sees blank stares from the employees. "Good. Thank you for attending." He hurriedly leaves the conference room while the employees stay put.

Later the same day, Charles Whitehead props his arms over his stomach, leans back in his chair and twists his nose a few times as he looks up at the ceiling.

There is a silence in the room that would feel eerie to most, but not to them. They've been through the routine many times before starting important conversations, and they know Whitehead must start it out. This time is no exception.

"There are only a few things worse than a funeral but mentioning them would only tear up your heart. Some people are asked to speak, while others aren't asked for very specific reasons. Those listening really aren't listening anyway to whoever says what they say, from the provocative and poignant to the stupid and silly. Yet, it's the process that seems to matter … don't disrespect the process. Most if not all people wear black out of observance while some hold tissues to their nose, sniffling softly but clearly heard by others. Some even hug each other, saying indistinguishable and unclear words to one another, rubbing each other's back and nodding their heads as if they've understood and agree with the other. Only a few people, especially the elderly, know that the feeling will pass, memories will drift away, and the world will go on. While people arrive at a funeral in dribs and drabs, most will leave at the same time, seemingly anxious to leave the gloomy environment. Only a few cultures do it right with celebrations, drinking, eating, and dancing that last several hours."

The relevance of his comments is not questioned by his son-in-law or the Chief Legal Counsel. They've learned it is of no use, and can easily upset him. It's Whitehead's way of thinking through issues.

Charles Whitehead drops his head to look at his longtime friend and confident, and then at his son-in-law. "This is an important decision. She clearly is aggressive and obviously knows how businesses compete in a market. What I don't know is her loyalty. Can she be trusted? Will she put her full allegiance to us? Can we depend on her to do what is right for the organization even if it rubs against her own set of values? I don't know."

Rose suggests, "We can have our people do an exhaustive background check on her, find out everything about her."

Charles replies, "That'll happen automatically. That's not what I'm concerned about."

His son-in-law politely asks, "Then what is it?"

Charles Whitehead grins, but not enough for the average person to pick up on it. "I'm talking about her dark side." He takes in a deep breath of air and slowly releases it back into the room. He looks at Rose first, holding his eyes on him for a few seconds, and then to his son-in-law. He drops his eyes for a split second and then continues as he alternatively gazes at each of them. "There's a fascination with the darkness, almost as if it is a love affair with someone you shouldn't be with for what it may hold. It's a combination of fear and uncontrolled pleasure for many, sort of a lure to taste it, to take the bait, even to feel and smell it. Darkness is forbidding but not enough for many of us to stay away. We are driven to the darkness if only for a moment or if for a lifetime. Consider our businesses, past and present. There were and are dark sides. We have to be one hundred percent sure we can trust her, that she will not betray us. If we bring her into the business, she'll know everything, which means we must trust her and she must trust us."

Rose responds. "I don't see a way to be one hundred percent certain of her. We don't know her. We've never worked with her. We don't know how she'll really respond to the temptations she'll face. We've never brought in someone from the outside to be this close to the business. We just don't know."

Charles asks his son-in-law, "And what are your thoughts? You've been quiet. She's about your age."

Fred is quick to answer. "I don't trust her. It's just a gut feeling. She's out for herself and will do anything to anyone to get it. The end will justify the means. She has a very dark side and I think it would be only a matter of time before we see it. I wouldn't take a chance on her."

Rose jumps in. "Unless we find out something about her that she wants to be kept secret, and will do anything to keep it that way. It would be our assurance."

Fred challenges the idea. "And there would be nothing to prevent her from finding out about our dealings if she becomes an insider. She'll have her assurance as we'll have ours … a stalemate."

Charles listens to the now deafening silence, glances at each of the men, settling on no one in particular. He smiles. "I want to take a chance on her, but not as part of our executive committee. Let her prove herself. What about having her report to you since you're the most skeptical?" He looks at his son-in-law.

There is a surprised look on Fred's face along with initial silence. He rolls his eyes.

Charles grins, "Do I take that as a yes?"

The son-in-law reluctantly nods in agreement.

Charles says, "It's settled. She's to report to you as the Senior Product Strategist for our current products. She can keep her current team but no additions or replacements unless we agree. Increase her current compensation plan by twenty-five percent. Let her stay in her current office.

Only give her information that helps her with that job only, nothing else. We'll throw in several tests along the way to gage her loyalty." He turns to Rose. "I want a complete criminal check on her done quickly. You know what I'm referring to."

Rose replies, "Felonies, misdemeanors, violations, fines, probation, prison time, drug possession - sale - use, possession of a deadly weapon, gross vehicular manslaughter, D.U.I., murder, robbery, grand theft and the like."

"Yes, yes. Am I missing anything else?" Charles looks around the room to see his son-in-law nod yes. "What is it?"

"What about money problems … alimony payments, child support, outstanding loans, gambling, and so on. And we should know about any former and current marriages, heath issues, psychiatric evaluations … you know, the whole shit and caboodle."

"Good. What else?" Charles looks around again to see heads' shake, no. "OK, then it's settled. Assuming nothing about her background is of our concern, let's bring her back in to work out the details."

Whitney confidently walks into the room with poise and assurance that implies she already knows the outcome. Her self-assuredness does not go unnoticed by the three men. She stops only a few feet from them, looks directly into each pair of eyes, a bold move by anyone's standards. She smells of recently applied perfume. She remains silent for a short time, yet internally moved by being invited to return. She notices that Charles Whitehead breaks into a quick yet sincere grin that for a short second confuses her as to what it might mean.

Then Whitehead speaks. "Please, come sit by me." He pats a chair that has been moved to be within inches of his chair.

Slowly and with certainty she complies. Once seated, she crosses her slender and elegant legs. She feels their eyes glow with enchantment, something that pleases her. Then she slowly turns her head to face each man, starting with Charles Whitehead, and articulating with as much charm as she can bring together, "Thank you for inviting me back." There is no panic or sense of urgency in her expression.

Whitehead picks his words carefully. "We've come to a joint conclusion that you're an important talent for our organization. You've demonstrated in a very short time your knowledge and passion for success." He pauses to look at his son-in-law and Rose, and then he returns to look at Whitney as he says to her, "Your background isn't a knockout factor to us, although somewhat out of the ordinary. There's nothing that worries us."

She remains quiet without any noticeable reaction, just listening carefully, but not acting as if she wants him to explain anything or to go faster, yet that is exactly what she wants. Instead, she knows he needs to talk at his own pace, safe and without any hurry. There is no point in trying to rush him to force him to say something he doesn't want to say. She gently smiles and slightly nods her head as she straightens her back to show her breasts, obviously braless.

Whitehead continues. "We'd like to have you join us as THE Senior Product Strategist for all our current products. This is a very important role, something that has been missing and can be done with your type of passion. We believe you're a very good fit. You'll be able to retain your current team but for the moment there cannot be any additions or replacements to your staff. Your current compensation plan will be increased by twenty-five percent, and you can retain your current office." He pauses, anticipating a question or some other kind of response.

"This is very satisfying." She grins with obvious pleasure and joy. "And do I report to you directly?"

Whitehead looks at his son-in-law and back to Whitney. "We all in a way report to each other, but there is a need for a formal organizational structure. I'm sure you understand." He waits to see how she responds.

Whitney nods her head once to signal an understanding. "Is it you, Mr. Rose or Mr. Saunders?"

Whitehead nods towards Saunders. "It is my son-in-law, Fred Saunders, who is the President."

Fred decides it's time to say something to his new employee. "I'm sure we'll have much to learn from each other. I'm definitely looking forward to the relationship." His voice is sufficiently soft to almost make him seem unseen.

She tries to hide her feelings, but her body reveals the truth as she fully turns his way to look at him in a gaze that is sensual. Slowly she crosses her legs for a second time to show off her beauty.

The two elder men in the room quickly pick up on Whitney's suggestive behavior but it is she and Fred who have clearly communicated.

Whitehead looks around at everyone. "If there isn't anything else to discuss, then Whitney needs to complete some paperwork and then she and her boss need to figure out a game plan." He sees yes nods from everyone. "Wonderful." He stands and reaches his right hand toward Whitney, "Welcome. I look forward to working with you."

Hank Rose steps forward to offer the same congratulations to Whitney.

Fred Saunders holds back to postpone his welcome. A moment of silence cuts through the air that signals to him it's his turn. He slowly steps forward towards Whitney with a similar handshake and tattered symbolic words. When he feels his hand in hers he is surprised that she squeezes it just a little and then releases her grip. A flash of heated emotion penetrates his body.

One week later, Hank Rose walks into the office of Charles Whitehead with a file on Whitney. The dossier is thick. "She's quite a woman, but there's nothing about her background that should be a concern to us. Do you want to know some of the details? You'll find it interesting and some of it even amusing that might make you laugh."

Whitehead looks up from his desk, signing legal documents previously prepared by Rose. He puts his black Mont Blanc fountain pen on the desk top, tilts his head backward just enough for the chair to slant backward. "I'm all ears."

"She's a lawyer by schooling, but never took the bar exam for some reason. Married once, husband took off to be with his boyfriend that shocked the hell out of her. She's been seen by a psychotherapist off and on but not steady since her husband left her. Her difficulties all seem to stem from the marital crisis."

Whitehead interrupts with a grin on his face. "No … really. I don't understand why." He turns his head from side to side. "I would have never thought." He pauses and then says, "Go on." He chuckles.

"Many of her personality traits are based on not easily adapting to conventional environments. She can be cold, rigid, excessively perfectionist, and preoccupied with the minutest of details. She is insistent on doing things her way and that others should change. She is excessively devoted to work. She carries on her sexual goings-on in the same manner." Rose pauses to discern if he should elaborate or move on.

Whitehead face breaks into a raucous fit of laughter that he can't hold back. "In other words she's delusional, narcissistic, and a sex-addict!"

Rose looks at him without the same facial expression. "I'm not a doctor, I wouldn't know."

"Go on." He cups the back of his head with the palms of his two hands. He grins.

Rose takes a look at the file. "While she drives people crazy with her personality, there are many who thrive on her style, in fact are one hundred percent devoted to her, such as the staff she now has. I'd be surprised if anyone of them would go against her directly or indirectly."

"They may too have some of her problems, but don't see it that way." Another pause and then Whitehead asks, "If that's it about her psychological condition, move on. As long as she isn't dangerous to others, like tipping towards physically harming someone, I can live with it. She's Fred's problem, not mine or yours."

"Should we forewarn him or let him figure it out himself."

"He's a big boy and a smart one at that. And while I don't want him to think we're meddling he should be told by you."

Rose takes another look at the file. "No kids or living family. No drinking problems. She's paid her taxes and has mostly been a law abiding citizen except for one run-in with the law. Just after her hubby ran off, she was stopped by two State Highway Patrol Officers on Interstate 5 for traveling 92 mph in a 65 mph zone and for changing lanes without signaling. It was 11 pm on a weeknight. Upon being requested to show her license and registration, she became hostile and verbally offensive towards the Officers. She was then asked to get out of her car and empty her pockets and purse. She complied. Four marijuana cigarettes were found by one of the Officers inside a regular looking brass cigarette case. The other Officer noticed a plastic bag in the back seat that upon inspection contained 2 ounces of heroin. She was then arrested. Bail was set at $6,000 which she met. At trial she was charged with violation of a health and safety code for the heroin, violation of a health and safety code for possession of the marijuana, and violation of a penal code for resisting, delaying, and obstructing Officers from doing their jobs. Possession of marijuana was and still is a Class A Misdemeanor that carried a maximum of 2 ½ years in jail with a fine of up to $1,000. Possession of heroin was and still is a Federal Offense that carried a maximum of 10 years in jail with a fine of up to $5,000. The Misdemeanor violation for resisting, delaying, and obstructing Officers from doing their job only carried a fine of up to $250 with possible probation. The speeding violation carried a fine of up to $400 with possible probation." He looks up at Whitehead with a grin. "What do you think she got?"

Whitehead smacks his lips. "In addition to the $6,000 bail, she was slapped with a warning, and paid the $650 total fine for interfering with the Officers' work and for speeding but without probation. Points were placed on her driving record that could have been removed if she took an online course, which I'll bet she refused." He grins, smacks his lips again, and asks "How did I do?"

Rose chuckles aloud. "You've earned an A-grade for accuracy."

"Does that do it, or have you left the best until last?"

"No. There's no more that should concern us."

"Nice work." Whitehead looks down at the remaining papers he needs to read and sign-off on. "I've got to get to these, so if there isn't anything remaining, thanks."

Rose silently looks at Whitehead whose unaltered neutral looking expression tells him that his boss has other work to attend to, and that his work is now finished. He turns and is about to leave Whitehead alone when he stops.

The unexpected motion alerts both men there is further business.

Rose says, "I know you're very busy and I wouldn't mention this unless I thought it was important. The F. B. I. has uncovered something we'd both prefer to be kept hidden."

Whitehead's mouth opens without any sound, an

obvious sign of surprise. He nods towards Rose to sit down. "Talk to me."

"Back when we were young, kids really, we both worked for some people who had a lot of influence in the neighborhoods," he ambiguously says knowing they both know what he's referring to. "If we knew then what we know now, it's not a world we'd both want any part of. But, we've, in a way, lived two different lives … then and now."

Whitehead interrupts. "What are you saying … that we were part of something criminal … organized crime?"

"I'm not saying that, no, I'm not. But the F. B. I. has stacks of documents that suggest otherwise. According to my sources, we have been linked to the Mafia when we did odds and ends at the Club, specifically to some people who have been and continue to be suspected of helping make certain people of nuisance disappear."

"You've got to be crazy!"

"No, I'm not the one who's crazy … it's the Bureau who has a thorn in their ass to dig up shit on people like us. There is a new President in place with his own Cabinet and other appointed Government officials who will want to make a name for themselves in order to show everyone how proactive and relentless they are on organized crime."

"The taxi situation job was inconsequential! Hell, we both almost got killed! We weren't even carrying guns ourselves!"

"The Bureau has another interpretation. They say that the entire industry was infiltrated by the Mafia at that time … that even juveniles like us profited."

"I um … I um … shit." Whitehead sits in silence for a few seconds … his mind spins as he stares at Rose who he doesn't even see at the moment. "It was a life that we did to help our families. Without the money, who knows what would have happened to them." He now sounds weak, pitiful, and miserable in order to rationalize the behavior. "We were exposed to bad things and corrupt people at a young age."

Rose subscribes to the same argument, although from a legal standpoint knows that if it came to a trial with a jury there would be no sympathy. "We got out, I know we did. We married respectable women from reputable families. We started businesses together and even donated money to help fix up properties and champion financial support for struggling families. We raised our families in a good environment. But you know exactly what I'm thinking about all of this."

Whitehead lets a full breath of air flow around in the room. "The Code was that there was no way of getting out. Once you were in, you stayed in."

"We should be prepared to be investigated once the new Administration is fully in place. It'll take a lot of work on their part since so much time has passed, and I don't know how high this priority will be on their Agenda. We need to stay strong. We've both survived worse conditions."

"I haven't thought about this in years, but I haven't forgotten about it. When you've been shot at you don't forget."

"Are you joking?" Whitney lies to her new boss, Fred Saunders, with her still body, no movement whatsoever, just an angry look that is incensed with resentment. But the sound of her voice is a giveaway, a snarl that is more sounding like a snapping sound.

"If I were, I'd be laughing."

Her feelings are now poorly disguised. She is hurt yet undeterred. She will not let the information shatter her life. She sits still. Now her breathing is heavy, nervous breaths, waiting for something more terrible to happen that she's tried to keep hidden for such a longtime.

He passes the report for her to read. "It's all here, all documented." He continues to stare at her. "It's obvious not at a level that concerns WRS, but it's who you are."

She reaches for the document and begins to read. After she finishes studying the entire document, she looks to her right towards the row of windows in his 12th floor office, and catches a reflection of herself but barely recognizes who she sees.

Saunders is unmoved by her realization. "It's the truth. It's who you are."

She feels an oversized spasm wanting to take control of her entire body that causes her to cling to the arms of the chair with as much might as possible. Her eyes are transfixed with a pain that she cannot hide.

"And don't for a second think you can fool me."

She tries one more time to deceive him. She yells, "I don't believe any of this!" She waves the document high in the air. "It's all fake information, fabricated to make me look dreadful!"

He leans forward in his chair. His voice is calm and monotone but there is an easily understood warning in it. "Whatever you've said or want to say, and whatever you have already done, I'll forgive you this time and this time only, but never again as long as you are honest with me from this point forward. If you dance with the devil, you'll get pricked by the horns. I hope I am clear."

She hears whispers in her ears … something is knocking at her door. She knows that by repeating the same behavior in hope that the results will be different is foolish. Slowly she looks directly at him. "Yes, I understand perfectly what you've said."

He breathes out a contented breath of air. "Truth is complicated and sometimes it is not what you believed it would be." He gives her a smile that is threated with a warning. "Now that we've got that settled, let's talk about your strategic business plan."

They start to speak to each other as if they are playacting, words and the sounds pretending to be from someone else. It has to be that way for now until they are able to fully trust one another, even if that is remotely possible.

For the time being, she no longer tries to run away from her own shadow, but like many things in life, planned and unexpected change happens. Yet, it's tough to change what you've repeatedly been doing for a while.

One hour later Whitney leaves Saunders' office feeling more comfortable about her role in the new organization. She thinks to herself that she can see a long term future there. As she steps into the hallway she checks her cellphone for any calls she might have missed during the hour-long meeting. One in particular catches her attention so she retrieves the call as she walks into a far corner of the hallway and turns her back away from the elevators. She listens.

"Client 7152TD, your 9 pm appointment with Mathew has changed due to his illness. We wouldn't want you to catch his cold. We're prepared to substitute Mathew with Jesse. You won't be disappointed with Jesse. Just confirm at your earliest time. Thank you." She frowns, disappointed about Mathew's absence, but eager to experience someone new. As she confirms, a woman walks past her. Whitney, with her head tilted towards the floor can only make out her shoes … black classic T-strap style office shoes that look stylish and sexy to her. Whitney finishes the quick confirmation of Jesse for tonight, and then she walks towards the elevator to take her to the 9th floor for a planned meeting with her employees.

As she steps into a large conference room she is excited to see so many employees. She scans the crowd without making direct contact with anyone at first as they look directly at her … about half she figures are from her prior job while the other half are from another department that has merged with her prior one. She waves to everyone. "Hello. Welcome to your new home." All eyes are squarely pointed her way. "I'm so proud to be working with each and every one of you. The new ownership is 100 percent committed to supporting us and making WRS greater than anyone can ever imagine. Working together as a team is all I ask."

The conference door at the right side of the room suddenly opens. A woman enters, trying her best to go unnoticed but her attempt fails miserably as everyone looks her way. The woman wears shoes that Whitney just recently noticed on the 12th floor. Her mind spins to a quick conclusion … it had to be her.

"I'm very sorry I'm late." The woman's voice is shy with a noticeable nervousness. She takes a seat quickly and keeps her head tucked downward to avoid eye contact.

Whitney swallows and then continues where she left off. "Many of you know me while some of you may have only heard of me. And, it's quite possible that a few may not know who I am. Regardless, we're going to create great success for WRS and for each of you. I can be intense at times."

There are a few hushed chuckles from the crowd.

She continues. "And, some of you already know what I mean." She grins as she wiggles her eyebrows looking at the few who chuckled. "I expect you to be committed to both WRS's mission and to ours as well. If you don't understand something, you have to ask me. I can take good news as well as bad news. But I can't take no news. So bring me your problems early and I'm your partner, but if you bring me your problems late I'm your judge. I just left the President's office giving him our Plan. He loves it and is fully behind it with all necessary funding. The Plan has been posted on our Intranet site so you can read it. In a few days, definitely by the end of week, we'll meet again to discuss your specific roles. To prepare for that meeting, I'll want each of you to specifically identify what you offer … what your role should be … what resources you'll need … and how it all supports the Plan. That meeting will last most of the day so be prepared. If I were in your shoes now, I'd read the Plan immediately so that you can recite it." Whitney slowly turns her head to focus on each person, one at a time, nodding each time she latches onto their eyes with hers. "Are there any questions?"

All of her former employees stand up together as if they had planned it out. They clap and yell, "Hurrah!" in unison. Then quickly, the rest of the employees join in the celebration.

At exactly 9 pm that evening, her apartment doorbell rings. She smiles, knows who's waiting. Dressed in loose fitting clothes without shoes, she walks towards the intercom, presses a button. "Yes?"

"If you are Client 7152TD, then I am Jesse."

A broad grin emerges on her face that stays a while as if she is a little girl waiting to open up a birthday gift. She presses a button that allows Jesse into the apartment building. She nods her head with great anticipation, looks at the door awaiting a knock. The wait is short.

She slowly opens the door to look at the handsome 6 foot man standing, dressed in blue jeans, boots, and a tight fitting black shirt. His hair is cut short, almost military style without any facial hair. She figures he probably weighs 200 pounds of solid muscle. His smile is broad and his teeth are perfect and pearly white. She is pleased, very pleased. She calls him by his first name believing it is not real ... to make their union more impersonal, to keep a certain distance between them. But this time it is more ... the way she says it ... eerie in a way that seems to suggest she wants a real connection to someone genuine she can trust. "Hi, Jesse, come on in."

She steps aside just enough that their bodies rub against each other.

He stops, and then slowly moves his hips in just the right way to meet her lower extremity.

She pushes the door closed with one hand and then envelops his neck with both hands. He smells of coconut oil. As they kiss she unzips his jeans to grab hold of him.

He reciprocates with a quick undressing of her.

Now, both naked, they devour each other in unrelenting sex until each of them has nothing left to give or to take. They flop over on the floor, still encircled in each other's bodies, quiet and content for the time being.

CHAPTER 3

It is 2 in the morning as her eyes pop open. Jesse is curled up against her in a quasi-fetal-like position. She feels not only his piece of equipment touching her but she feels tired and her throat is sore for some reason ... really? Please. So what if she's been asleep for less than 4 hours. That's nothing new. In fact, it seems as if it is becoming the new normal for her.

She squirms away from him ... he rolls to his other side, legs still bent up towards his chest. He's still sleeping like a baby. She's got to get him out of her place to get ready for work so she slightly-more-than shoves him with her foot.

"Hey, time to go!" She doesn't give him any time to think about what happened between them. Yes, it was satisfying ... very much so ... but priorities are priorities and they have just changed. "Hey, get up, time to go!" She uses her foot a little more aggressively this time.

Jesse slowly rolls her way, stretches his arms over his head and yawns. He looks at her ... a bit dazed by the sudden and unwelcomed morning wake up. "Huh?"

"Sergeant, it's time to go." She nods for him to get on with it. You've got to know what's important and what's trivial, she silently reminds herself.

He knows the drill and doesn't argue. Jesse slowly

stands, reaches for his clothes that have been wildly scattered on the floor. As he dresses he can't help but momentarily stare at her beautiful body, still mostly naked. A grin takes over his face.

She places an envelope on a nearby chair. "There's a nice thank-you inside. I'm gonna be sure to see you again. You might just have replaced Mathew." She turns to walk away. "I've got to get ready for work. You know where the door is. Make sure it is closed when you leave."

She's already planning the day's work. Priority one is to make it known she doesn't tolerate spies of any kind. The girl with the cute shoes she saw on the President's floor has to go. Number two is to assign Karen, her most trusted and loyal employee, the task of building and managing a Company Blog. She has several ideas and is convinced that Karen has some good ones herself.

Whitney focuses on staying in the moment, not intending to allow a cold, a nervous breakdown, an act of compassion, or anything else to get in her way. Once she sticks the oar in the water, there's no turning back. She's not turning tail to return to Schenectady. She takes in a deep breath of air to get a grip, to take her own advice, to set aside any shit that is and will be thrown her way. She's the only one she can rely on one hundred percent of the time … she can't … won't … let herself down. Whitney is now alone in her apartment. She heard the door shut … Jesse left but will definitely return when she's ready to be sexually satisfied. She grins.

She pops a throat lozenge into her mouth to sooth the discomfort ignoring that the soreness could be something else. She grimaces at the taste of the tablet.

She looks at herself in the bathroom mirror as she brushes her hair, followed by minimal makeup to her natural smooth unblemished skin. Then she notices a slight bruise on the right side of her neck … more like the beginning of a swell that is puffed out. Did she and Jesse get that physical? Quickly ignoring the cause she craftily covers it with a slight brush of makeup. She really doesn't want to know how it happened, at least not now. There are more important matters needing her attention. She is not going to think about what may or may not have happened between Jesse and her … that's on hold for now. What's really important is what's going to happen today at the office. She finishes her grooming tasks, takes a final look at herself in the mirror and approves of who she sees, gives herself a thumbs-up, and heads for the apartment door.

About to pick up her keys that lay on a small table, Whitney notices the same envelope she left for Jesse that is now void of the generous bonus for a job well done. Handwritten on the front side of the empty envelope is printed a question mark inside of a heart-shaped figure. She chuckles.

Upon entering the ground floor lobby of the Office building she notices the security guards intently looking at her. Their look is of deference to her, a nod of the head, a smile, and even a slight bow. For an instant Whitney thinks she's been transformed to another space-dimension on another planet, but she quickly is brought back to earth when she hears from one of the security guards.

"Miss Danica, good morning. It's good to see you. Is there anything any of us can do for you today?"

For another instant ... a rare instant ... Whitney is without words, but quickly recovers. "Thank you. I'm fine. I hope all of you have a fine day." She starts to walk directly to the bank of elevators.

She must have made an impression on all of them because all of a sudden each and every security guard seems to be standing at military attention as if she is a Queen.

"Miss Danica, over here ... please."

Her eyes widen as she notices a security guard motioning her way, indicating her to take another elevator to her office. She thinks, momentarily, there must be some mistake. She stands still with a frown.

The security guard straightens out her temporary confusion. "This elevator is reserved for your private use. It takes you directly to your new office."

There is no mistake. Whitney's heart pounds a little faster and harder. She thinks to herself, could this really be happening to me?

Later on at midday, Whitney and her most trusted employee, Karen, discuss blogging.

Whitney is excited, enthusiastic about the whole idea of starting a Blog for WRS. Not only does the sound of her voice but the animation of her body convey a convincing argument to Karen who listens carefully. "You're going to create a buzz within the industry, despite the resistance from those still frozen in old school marketing. Nothing like this has ever been done, especially at this level. You're the pioneer … the first ever!"

Karen sits in a chair across from her boss, excited as well that Whitney thought of her first to take on the project. "I'm on cloud nine just thinking about it. In a time when it seems everyone is online for one thing or another, a Company Blog can create a personalized voice to its current customer base, as well as be a reach-out tool to bring in new customers. This is going to make people dizzy!"

"Remember, the information needs to be repeated over and over again … there has to be opportunity for our current customers to interact with you … specialize your messages, each and every one of them … keep the messages focused and narrow, no tangents … only use credible data that has been critically analyzed … you'll probably need additional help, so pick anyone from the Department, just tell me who … use your own natural and personalized voice … I want the market to believe they know you as a real person."

"Yeah, yeah," Karen breathlessly calls out as she keeps up her note taking as Whitney talks.

Whitney continues. "Down deep inside, people want to be told … they really don't want to think too much about what product to buy. They don't have the patience to do their own homework. Maybe they're just too lazy or have too much on their plate. I really don't know the reason, but I know the answer. Remember, Karen, millions and millions of people will be counting on you!"

As Karen continues to take notes, her smile continues to be enthusiastic that is both broad and sincere. Then she stops, leans back in the chair and takes in a deep breath of needed air as if she just finished running a hundred yard sprint. "Is there anything else before I jump into it?"

Whitney puckers her lips before saying in a low and monotone voice, "Not on this topic ... something else."

Karen's face suddenly becomes serious, taken by surprise. Her eyebrows are now slightly raised. She starts to play with the ballpoint pen with her fingers, and almost drops it in her lap, but clenches it in the nick-of-time. "Oh?"

Whitney leans forward, comfortable in answering. Her voice is lowered although there is no one else in the office to overhear the conversation. "There was a female about your age who walked in late at the meeting. She was wearing black classic T-strap style office shoes ... fashionable."

Karen waits for more information but when none comes, she asks, "What about her?"

"Do you know her?"

"Indirectly, she was part of the other Department that merged with ours. What else do you want to know?"

"Her name, what's her name?"

"Lynda, uh – uh – what is it? Lynda ... Lynda ... Ackerman. Yeah, that's her name, Lynda Ackerman."

"What else?"

"Not much that I know. I think she was recently hired, about a month or less. Don't know what her job skill is or what she did with them." Karen shakes her head from side to side to reinforce limited information. "Can I ask why you want to know? Do you want to know where she bought her shoes? Is that it?"

"No, not that, but something else." Whitney hesitates wondering if she should divulge anything more to Karen. Maybe the less she knows the better it is. She looks directly into Karen's inquisitive eyes and then confides. "I saw her walk towards the President's office the other day as I was leaving. I was standing by the elevator when she – Lynda – passed me. I just have an uncomfortable feeling … something strange that I can't put my finger on. That's all. Maybe it's nothing."

Karen keeps looking at Whitney without a blink. "You're worried about something. It may be none of my business, so I'm not gonna pry. But, if you want me to check around without anyone noticing I can."

Whitney breathes out a slight sigh of relief, almost imperceptible to most people, but not to Karen. "Well, since you asked … that would be helpful. Don't let anyone know … I wouldn't want to worry anyone."

"No problem." Her voice is monotone, yet when she feels her upper lip start to quiver, she quickly places her hand over her mouth. She knows something serious is up and she won't disappoint her boss.

Later the same day, Whitney leaves the Office. It is 9:44 pm and she stands on the sidewalk just outside the Office building thinking of whether to go for a drink at one of her usual places or go on home. She could really use a good night's sleep. She looks around as if something will pop out of the sky to usher her to make a decision.

A dark colored four-door sedan pulls up nearby. A conservatively dressed man in a dark colored business suit, white shirt with black tie and black shoes steps out of the vehicle. "Whitney Danica?" His voice is northeastern

sounding, could be upstate New York, maybe even
Schenectady.

Her stomach sinks, expecting something very bad is
going to happen to her. She feels her stomach growl and
then all of a sudden he is by her side with a strong clamp of
her arm in his hand, a vice-like grip that doesn't let go. "Let
me go!" She shakes but is not able to loosen his grip. "Let
go of me!" She yells again, looks around to see if anyone is
near enough to come to her aid. She is only alone with the
man and whoever might else be in the car. She is very close
to freaking out but since she's had a full day of work, she's
very tired even to panic, but her personality won't let anyone
get the best of her regardless of the situation.

"Whitney Danica?" he asks a second time.

She now looks at him directly into his eyes, full face-
to-face. She thinks he's got law enforcement written all over
him but those aren't the type of men she spends time with.
"Who wants to know?" She juts out her chin in defiance.

"F. B. I.," he says.

She feels the loss of his grip. Did she make that happen
or did he do it without help? No longer panicky, thinking
that something terrible that was going to happen will not,
she lets out a breath of air.

"Are you Whitney Danica?"

His piercing black eyes are hard to look away from.
"Maybe, what do you want?"

"We'd like to talk with you about some people you
know."

"We, did you say we? Who are we?" She now notices
his black hair combed straight back, and a quite handsome

looking face without any facial hair. Things are going to be OK now, she thinks to herself.

"There's someone in the car who would like to talk with you. I'm Special Agent Scott Marin." He shows her his I.D. badge.

She takes a long look at it, never having seen a real one before. She's always used the ones you buy at novelty stores for her sexual foreplay.

"You are Whitney Danica, right?"

She figures he already knows the truth so why try to deny it. "Yeah, that's me."

"We'd like to ask you a few questions about some people you know. It shouldn't take long."

Whitney shrugs her shoulders, "Who?"

His fingers quickly return to her arm. As they clamp down harder now than the first time, the back door of the sedan opens. "We'll tell you inside."

In spite of his firm grip, Whitney leans over to spot a female sitting inside, professionally dressed in similar dark conservative clothes like her partner.

"Miss Danica, I'm Special Agent Paula McEwen. Please join me. I promise it will not take long."

It takes Whitney a split second to make up her mind. "Sorry, but I've already got plans … and come to think of it, I'm late as it is now … maybe some other time." Her voice is cool, calm, and collected.

McEwen nods to Marin resulting in Whitney being forced into the backseat of the car that quickly drives off.

With Whitney crowded between Marin and McEwen the black color sedan continues to drive away. She finds the nearness of the two Special Agents uncomfortable making it difficult for her to breath. She slowly tries to regain composure.

"Thank you for agreeing to talk with us." McEwen's voice sounds as if it is from someplace in the South.

"Be serious, did I really have a choice?" Whitney tries to mimic McEwen's sound but fails miserably.

"You've got to be from New Orleans to sound like you're from New Orleans." McEwen grins in a way that cannot be interpreted as anything but sarcastic.

"Go to hell," Whitney says in a hushed voice that no one else can hear, but only can suspect.

"You're welcome." McEwen keeps up the sarcastic grin. "But we have more important matters than to provoke each other. So, how well do you know Mr. Charles Whitehead, his son-in-law Fred Saunders, and Mr. Hank Rose?" She looks straight ahead toward the front of the car without giving any consideration to Whitney.

"Are you investigating them?"

"I'll ask the questions." McEwen shifts her body to directly face Whitney resulting in even more closer proximity of one another.

For the first time Whitney notices the hazel color of her eyes that is oddly contrasted to her rich chocolate brown skin tone, something that is quite attractive to her liking. For a brief moment the two women's eyes stay glued to each other.

"Since when does the F. B. I. care about stuff like that?"

"Since now," McEwen replies.

Whitney figures the quickest way to end the uncomfortable situation and ultimately to be left alone is to answer a few innocuous questions. She commits to herself to make it brief and get right to the point as fast as possible. "They represent the new owners of WRS who recently bought out the Company I previously worked for. I met the three men for a short time after the buy-out just a few days ago. I suspect the Company's name has something to do with each of their last names, but that's just my hunch." She shrugs her shoulders and then continues. "It seems they decided to keep me employed for some odd reason. I hope they noticed my exceptional knowledge, skills and abilities. Come on, what other reason could there be?" She shrugs her shoulders again as she quickly turns to glance at Marin who has essentially been silent since he abducted her, and then back to McEwen. "That's it."

McEwen asks, "Do you know anything about their backgrounds … who they are, what they've done, the history of the Company, you know the stuff I'm talking about?"

"A big nope."

McEwen asks, "Why's that? Isn't a curious woman like yourself interested in those kinds of things?"

"I see that you need a few lessons in corporate America, you know the institutions that make America great … that pay taxes that pay your salaries … you know … that kind of stuff." She can't resist smirking … it feels so good. "It's the usual protocol for the employer to ask the questions of the candidate … in this case an employee of the company that's just been purchased, not the other way around. One could ask probing questions to the employer … I mean that's not really so unusual, but the bottom line is the person wanting to work for a company has to align with the mission, values, culture, etc. of the employer … not the other way around." Whitney feels more confident. Her stomach is no longer growling. She feels as if it's 'Game Time' and it really feels good to her.

Marin now enters the conversation. "I sense a little sarcasm."

As Whitney turns to face him she senses he's moved closer to crowd her even more firmly than before. Their eyes glare at one another. "I wonder why?" She has the urge to say more but smartly declines the inclination. She feels the muscles twitching beneath the skin of her hands.

His voice is calm. "And now ... hostility."

"Look, I'd really like to buy the both of you a drink or two to get to know you a bit more. I think you'd find me a really nice person who you'd want to send a birthday card and perhaps a Christmas card if you're inclined. But, really, I've got to go. What will it take for you to stop this freaking interrogation and car so that you disappear from my life?"

McEwen hands over to her a card with her name and a phone number. "In case you remember anything, give me a call."

Whitney looks at the card, about to toss it away, but then reconsiders. "I doubt it, but you never know."

McEwen taps the driver of the car on the shoulder.

Suddenly the car pulls off the road to the curb, not far from where Whitney was originally picked up.

Marin exits the car, steps aside to allow Whitney to exit.

After Whitney exits the car, Marin re-enters and drives off.

A short time later, Whitney stares at the mostly empty wine glass at the bar, the third Chardonnay within the hour.

No longer does she smell the alcohol or even taste it, but that's been her intent all along.

"You want coffee?" the bartender asks.

Her lips are mostly shut and her head is tilted downward so she doesn't see him. "No," she lies.

"Just trying to be helpful."

She looks up just enough to see his face. "I don't recognize you."

"Nor me with you."

"And …?"

"New shift for me. Sure you don't want some coffee, just recently brewed?"

"You're sure one hell of a talkative bartender," she answers still with a slightly tilted head towards him.

"It's part of the job description. I can't change it." He continues to clean the top of the bar with a cloth. The two empty glasses of Chardonnay she's already consumed and anything else she might drink from is kept separate and uncontaminated from all other drinking glasses, cups, or anything else that touches her mouth. His client just wants it that way, and he isn't about to ask any questions. Although, he thinks to himself, they're after her D.N.A. for some reason.

Whitney blurts out. "I just got an unexpected visit from the F. B. I. who thought I knew something about someone." She's surprised the information came out so easily, so she continues. "I had no idea what the hell they were after."

The bartender keeps listening. That too is part of the job description and his other real job.

Whitney continues. "At first I was shocked when they first asked, then I was mad when they kept at it, and now I don't give a damn!" Be careful she warns herself. Maybe the bartender is also F. B. I.? She looks up at the good looking man. Six feet plus, desert brown skin with deep piercing brown eyes, short black hair almost in an old fashion crewcut style, with a firm chin. Nothing about him tells her he is part of law enforcement, but how would she know, that's not the type of people she hangs out with?

He asks, "What do you plan to do?" While he's surprised she's talking about her recent experience so readily, he now understands the importance of what he needs to do next.

She gazes at him, picks up the almost empty glass of wine and swallows it with a single gulp. She sets the now empty glass on the bar. "I'm done. What do I owe you?"

"It seems as if you're still quite upset." He needs to keep her around for a little longer to complete his job. She's the title role while he's only a minor antagonist to the story.

"Really?" The sarcasm is once again obvious.

"So, you're afraid to go to the cops." It's a statement more than a question.

She frowns and then narrows her eyes. "The cops! Be serious, for all I know they could be in cahoots with the F. B. I.. They could even be behind it. Maybe even you." She lowers her eyes towards the bar.

"Seriously?" He finds it easy to talk with her and for a spit second is hesitant in finishing his part of the job. He hurriedly gets out of feeling any sort of sympathy for her, his target.

"How the hell do I know, but yeah, very?"

"What about the media --- you know, the papers, television, radio?"

"I can't prove anything. It's all my suspicion, my opinion.

I'm nobody and they'd never believe me." She pauses. "And why do you care anyway?"

"Maybe you're paranoia." He ignores her question.

"Thanks for the vote of confidence."

"You know what I mean." He smiles.

She takes a deep breath ... slow and purposeful ... to regain some composure without crying. She doesn't want to lose it ... to break down, but all is for naught as tears come to her eyes and slowly drip down her face lingering on her cheeks.

His gaze sweeps over her but since her eyes face the top of the bar, she does see his sympathetic look, and therefore is not interested in saying anything more. She stays quiet.

Not sure what else he can do, he forces a sincere grin, "Are you sure you don't want that cup of coffee?"

She pops her eyes towards him to now see his genuine concerned face, but is still confused. She wonders why this stranger ... a bartender she's never met before .... is so persistent about what's happened to her. Is he really coming onto her or is it simply her imagination working overtime? And further, what is it with the coffee thing. Is he interested ... really interested ... in knowing more about her? Her stomach clenches, her lips press together, and her heart picks up a beat. "OK," she says in a spur-of-the-moment way, and then immediately hating herself for giving in so easily. She meets his gaze head-on as if she is searching his face for something. She brushes off what she thinks are idle thoughts, but she shouldn't ... her instincts are very accomplished ... she should trust her instincts, especially now.

His grin is peaceful looking. Then he turns to reach for

an empty coffee cup. With his back turned to her he asks, "Cream or sugar?" He starts filling the cup. With hands as quick as a magician he drops a pellet into the cup.

It is a one word answer, "Black."

He sets the full cup of coffee in front of her without further comment, just looking at her in the same serene manner.

She reaches to take a sip. While not particularly hot or even tasty, she feels the burst almost immediately. She takes a second sip.

"I can call you a cab if you need one."

She wonders again if he's working up to volunteering to drive her back to her apartment, or maybe to his place for a little sex play. She takes in a deep breath of air after the third sip. "I'm good." She shakes her head sideways, no. It's over she tells herself. There is no way she's going to fall for this pitiful pickup line.

"Fair enough," he nods. "Let me know when you want the final tab." He moves about two feet away from her to continue drying a glass with a towel.

"Now is good."

Their gazes meet again, and are held for the last time. Then he walks away to prepare her final tab.

She reminds herself that she's always been good at playing her hand in demanding times ... using her best card, although she really doesn't like the metaphor. She'd like to believe that life is not a game of chance, but the truth is she relies on it ... it is all about chance.

She steps outside the bar, takes in a deep breath of

air and then looks both ways. She feels a little woozy, but attributes the lightheadedness to a buildup of stress in her life. She takes one further step thinking movement will clear it up, but she's mistaken. She suddenly falls to the sidewalk.

Simultaneously a twentyish aged couple walks hand and hand towards her. They see her fall. Call it karma or something else. The male uses his cell to call 911 as his girlfriend rushes to Whitney's side.

The girl leans over to touch Whitney. "Are you OK?"

"I – I don't know what came over me." Her speech pattern is slurred.

"I'm a nurse. We've called 911 and you'll be taken to a hospital just to be sure."

"No, no, I'm good. It's just … well … crap that's going on in my life right now. I'm OK." Her eyes flicker without seeing much.

The nurse looks into Whitney's eyes, more of an examination than a simple look. "Just to be sure, I'm an E.R. nurse."

Doctor Emily Grace smiles at Whitney who remains lying flat on an E.R. cot. There is noise everywhere as other patients are being admitted at the same time with a limited staff of E.R. Doctors, Nurses, and Physician Assistants to attend to their emergency medical needs. "Our examination preliminarily does not show any obvious cause of your lightheadedness. There are no external bruises, broken bones, or the like. Blood test results won't be ready until tomorrow morning. We'd want to do a C.A.T.-Scan as well. To be on the safe side it is my medical opinion that you be admitted to the Hospital for further observation. It's the safest thing to do. OK?"

"I'm OK, really." She begins to lift her head off the cot but a blast of dizziness forces her to drop back. She closes her eyes for a second and reopens them. A blurry image of Doctor Grace is all she can see.

"I think it's best you remain overnight." In spite of the commotion typically found in E.R.'s, Doctor Grace remains calm and her smile helps soothe Whitney into agreement.

Whitney's sleep is restless with urges just to get up and leave the Hospital room. Yet each time she pops her head up from the bed, her dizziness returns. So she finally decides to wait it out until the next morning. She finally falls asleep at 2 am, but 5 hours later is awakened by a Nurse.

"Good morning Miss Danica. How are you feeling today?" Nurse McBride's calm voice and sweet smile is what everyone should hear when they wake up.

Whitney slowly opens her eyes, breathes in with the same rate of speed, and smacks her lips. Her mouth is dry. "Ugh." She rubs the back of her fingers over her forehead as if she is working something through. Then she drops her eyes to her chest, and then up to see Nurse McBride.

"Here, let me help you take a drink of water. You're probably a little dehydrated." The Nurse walks closer to Whitney. She lifts a full glass of water that presently rests on a close night stand to aid Whitney in the process. "Take small sips."

Once finished, Nurse McBride holds onto the empty glass of water. "Doctor Silva has just started his rounds and should be with you shortly. So, just try to rest until he comes. OK?" She smiles again.

Whitney nods her head in agreement, and then the Nurse leaves her alone.

Whitney feels isolated and afraid … a tidal exhaustion almost smothers her body. Her mouth is dry again. There is no one around to care for her, other than the obvious medical practitioners in the Hospital, but she's not thinking of them … she's thinking that there's really no one in her life to care for her … to pray for her … to protect her. Maybe Karen might fit into the category but Whitney is too tired to make contact. Or, maybe Karen and others have tried to call her at her apartment … to find out why she isn't at work by now. Maybe they even called around to all the hospitals to see if she's been admitted for one reason or another, and when they finally found out where she was they were told that she couldn't have any visitors at the moment … strict Doctor's orders. Maybe ….

Her inner thoughts are interrupted when she hears her name called out.

"Miss Danica?"

She looks at the door to see a man in a white smock standing.

"I'm Doctor Silva." As he slowly walks her way he reviews her medical chart in his hands. He grabs a chair to move close to her. "How are you feeling this morning?" While his smile is genuine enough, it doesn't match anywhere close to Nurse McBride.

Whitney says, "I'm exhausted and my mouth is dry."

"I see. What about any aches or pains?"

She frowns at the Doctor's intuition or is he that good. "Yeah, my bones feel stiff and are a little aching."

"Anything else?" He now looks thoughtful at her, but not in a scary way.

She hesitates, not all sure about how to express her physical condition. She breathes in and out slowly.

He helps her out. "What about scratchy or prickly feeling skin or head hums?"

She thinks for a short time, "Yeah, that too."

He jots down a few notes on her medical record.

"What's going on with me?" Her voice is somber sounding.

He looks up. "You'll be OK, but you should stay with us for at least another full day, just for observation."

"What's happened to me?" She now sounds worried as if it is life-threatening.

He takes in a deep breath of air through his nose and then slowly releases it from his opened mouth. His voice is calm and serious sounding. "The blood tests indicate poisoning."

Whitney can't believe what she's heard. Her eyes bulge wide and her mouth opens without uttering a word.

Doctor Silva decides that while Whitney is shocked to hear of the news, she's also owed a more complete answer. "You'll be OK, so don't worry. There were low levels of lead and arsenic in your blood, not at a level to do any permanent harm, but sufficient to cause the symptoms you've felt and are still feeling. The likelihood is these amounts will diminish over time, but there could be residues lasting for a while. You are otherwise in good health ... in fact I'd say very good health ... which lets me be confident to say that there shouldn't be any permanent damage, thus allowing for a full recovery."

Whitney tries to process it all but her thoughts get in her own way. Her thinking is not as fast as she'd like it to be and now she jumps to the conclusion that she'll never be who she used to be. She'll be vulnerable and never again invincible. She coughs and tries to reach for the nearby glass that is empty.

Doctor Silva stands to retrieve the glass but when he discovers it empty he reaches for a nearby pitcher to fill it. Then he hands the full glass of water to Whitney. He watches her slightly trembling hands clasp the vessel and then slowly bring it to her mouth for a few swallows, and then hands it back to him.

She closes her eyes as she says, "Thanks Doc. I've some things to think about." A glimmer of a smile crosses her face. But then, something within her internal alarm system flashes. "What's wrong?"

The Doctor turns on a light switch that brightens a small x-ray machine close by on a nearby wall within the patient's room. Then he pulls out an x-ray he's been holding onto inside a manila folder. He jams the x-ray into the machine. "Look here." He points to a small spec between her shoulders. "It's very small. See?" He points directly at the diminutive spot.

Whitney squints, not sure what she's supposed to be looking at, "No, not really." She stretches her neck to get a clearer look. "What am I looking for?"

"I performed some routine preliminary x-rays of your upper body. I just wanted to be sure there weren't any broken bones, ligament tears or bruising. I wasn't suspecting anything, just being cautionary." While still looking at the x-ray he pauses for a second before continuing. "It's an old ... and I do mean very old ... microchip that was implanted many years ago when you were no more than one or two. The chip was probably injected with a syringe ... simple and painless."

Whitney opens her mouth wide, but there is no sound.

Doctor Silva continues without looking towards Whitney. "It's no longer working. In fact, it may never have worked. It's one of the earliest models ever experimented with. The problem during those early days was with faulty tellers, in other words search-detecting technology ... defective from the get-go. Secondly, was the coding ... not very sophisticated, but those were the early days. There were scores of experiments ... some funded and some not ... some medically sound and some not ... some morally valid and some not. You get the idea."

"Are you saying this is now inside me?"

"Yes, here, see it." He points again to a tiny spot between her shoulders. "This is an implant. I can't really tell much about it unless I inspect it ... either through scanning the item before it is removed from your body or after the minor surgery to remove it I might find some identification on the item itself."

"I still don't understand."

"First were transmitters, R.F.I.D., which means Radio Frequency Identification. They were used to track assembly line products. Then they progressed to tracking pets and livestock instead of using a hot branding iron."

"You said 'first.' What came next?"

"Later on technologists started to experiment with

implanting small devices within the human body that could detect early signs of diseases. Breast cancer was their first target, and if that proved successful then there would be more research to detect other forms of fatal diseases."

"Sounds like A.I.."

"Precisely ... this was the early use of artificial intelligence to try to collect data on patients to help detect diseases."

"But why me, did I have any proclivities towards fatal diseases?"

"I wouldn't know." He pauses. "Are your parents alive?"

"I don't know. I've never met them."

"So you don't know if either or both of them had or have any fatal diseases?"

"Yeah, that's right."

"Any other family members ... how about them?"

"Dido."

"Were you sick as a child ... maybe needing constant medical treatment or such during emergencies? Did you tend to get lost, run away, and not find your way back home? Anything like that?"

"Not that I remember."

"What about your parents? If they didn't tell you about the implant, then I wonder why they would do this."

"That's what I'm now asking." She pauses. Her face is close to being drained of color. "Maybe somebody else did?"

"Like who?"

"I don't know."

Doctor Silva asks, "And for what reason?"

"This is crazy!" Her pasty white face doesn't change color.

"Do you remember any of your childhood?"

"Only that I moved around a lot … later found out that I was going from foster home to foster home."

"So you're saying you didn't know your biological parents?"

"Right … as well as all family members."

"Hmm," he says as he strokes his chin. "Do you want it removed?"

"What information does it contain?"

"Good question. I doubt it contains anything but I can't be sure unless I scan it again with a more sophisticated reader. But if that fails, then I can take it out and then scan it again, assuming there is something to read."

"Can you do that now?"

"Of course, if that's what you want. We have the equipment available in the Hospital."

"Then, let's do it."

The Doctor reaches for an R.F.I.D. reader inside a small pouch. He looks up at Whitney. "I'll first try to scan it so see if it can identify any data. I brought one along since I figured you want to find out. This is a Radio Frequency Identification Reader that is able to pick up frequencies." He smiles. "This won't take much time." He places a metallic oval receiver over the spot of the implant between her shoulders and waits less than a minute, "No, nothing, no information."

Whitney says, "Take it the hell out of my body."

"We can do this tomorrow morning. Removing it requires minor surgery … very simple. Can you stay overnight in the Hospital?"

"If that's what it takes, then yes." She pauses and then adds, "I want the chip after you remove it."

The Doctor grins, "Sure, whatever you want, it is yours … as a memento?"

"Partially, but also I just want to be safe."

The next morning after the minor surgery, Doctor Silva shows Whitney the chip. "It was lodged against a bone which could have prohibited collecting any data when I first tried to scan for data yesterday. Let me try again now that the chip is removed." He picks up a portable scanner that is more sophisticated than the one he used yesterday, and initiates the scanning process on the chip. He waits only a few seconds to read the scanner, "Nothing." He turns the chip over in his hand a few times looking at it closely. "Hmm, that's interesting."

"What?"

"I'm surprised I didn't see it after it was removed and cleaned up. There seems to be some sort of alpha-numeric sequence on the chip." He looks up towards the ceiling, almost ignoring Whitney for a short time, concentrating on trying to process the eye-opener. "It could be the factory number or something else. It could be a password of a bank account, or even a credit/debit card number, or almost anything else."

"Like the Fibonacci sequence?"

"Huh?" He looks at her.

"Never mind, let me have it."

Two days later, Whitney is back at work. No one asks where she's been, except for Karen. "You OK?"

"Oh yeah, fine, I just needed to hide away for a while to think though a few things. Thanks for asking."

"Anything I can do?"

"No, I can't think of anything now. Just keep doing what you've always been doing."

"I called your cell when you didn't show up for work."

"Yeah, I know," she lies. "I should have returned your call to say I was taking a few days off. I'm sorry."

"No worry. I'm just glad everything's OK."

"Yeah, I just needed a little rest … nothing more." Her voice is less than convincing this time.

"You seem a little different today. Maybe it was time well spent away from this place." Karen smiles but she suspects something else is up. She wonders if she should pursue it further or let it go. In the end she drops it.

"Yeah, that's probably it." She pauses to stare at Karen and then continues. "I don't think I've told you how much I appreciate you standing with me." She feels her throat slightly constrict so she coughs and then swallows deeply. "I know I can always count on you." Then, she takes another deep swallow.

Karen frowns just a bit recognizing a change in her boss. "And you've got my back as well." She touches Whitney's hand for reassurance.

There is a temporary halt in their atypical conversation.

Finally Karen breaks the silence. "Just as a reminder, you're got an afternoon meeting."

Whitney walks in the conference room. Four people are seated around a table, three of whom she recognizes as the C. E. O., President, and Chief Legal Counsel. However, the fourth person is a stranger to her. She glances at their eyes and quickly realizes with a sinking feeling something is wrong. Nobody is smiling. Nobody asks about her recent absence from work. Does anybody know? Does anybody care?

Hank Rose, the Chief Legal Counsel, is the first to speak. "We understand you had two visitors recently."

The unknown female, sitting straight and proper in her chair glances at the laptop screen facing her.

Whitney is sure she's never met the woman before, or even seen her until now, but she's as sure as hell believing the woman is important. She steps forward, toward her. "I'm Whitney Danica." I don't think we've met before." She keeps her gaze soft and non-threatening.

The woman remains quiet and motionless as Rose says, "She works for us … keeps track of certain things, like who sees who … reports to us about anything unusual or suspicious."

"I see," Whitney says yet it is unclear to her. She frowns.

The unknown woman's hair is dark brown and pulled straight back to match her rich blemish free skin tone that accentuates her brown oval eyes.

Rose continues, "What did they ask you?"

Whitney's grin is more like a smirk than a smile. She's not happy that she's been spied on. "Who are you talking about?" She tilts her chin upward in defiance, something that is not recommended to do with your boss present and especially with others in the meeting.

"The two people in the car … the woman and man … you know whom I referring to."

"Oh, them."

"Yes, them."

"Who were they? I don't think they ever told me who they were." She lies.

"You know who they were. F.B.I. … snooping." His voice is stern.

"Oh yeah, that's right. They did mention something like that."

Rose now sounds a bit impatient with her evasiveness. "Damn it, what did they ask you?"

Whitney pauses to add to her guile. Then she answers, "If I knew anything about the three of you that might interest them." She fights the urge to wet her lips.

"And what did you say?"

"To go to hell," Whitney wiggles her eyebrows. "They should ask you, not me!"

It is clear that her facial expression impressed them as they all chuckle in unison except for the unknown woman who remains stone-faced.

Rose asks, "This is a privately held Company, and that's the way we want to keep it."

Whitney nods to agree, "Of course. Given what happened a few nights ago, you have nothing to worry about as it pertains to me. I'm as loyal as they come."

There is a pause in the conversation as Rose looks to Charles and then to Fred.

Fred Saunders speaks as if the topic is now put to rest, "On another subject. Tell us about creating a Company Blog. It sounds promising."

Pleased the topic has changed, at least for the time being, Whitney answers. "The name of the game in today's market place is attracting attention. If people don't know much or anything about you, then you don't exist. It's a simple principle overlooked by many companies, even those with great products and services. Research has shown this time and again."

"Hmm," Fred says.

Whitney continues. "And that's where the Company Blog comes into play. I've assigned the design and implementation plan of a Company Blog to my top employee, Karen O'Leary. Within a week we'll have something specific to propose that will knock your socks off."

Charles Whitehead says, "Yes, of course."

Whitney sneaks a look at Rose and the unknown woman who remain expressionless.

The other two men nod in agreement.

Then Rose jumps in. "Given what happened … or didn't happen … a few nights ago we apparently don't have to worry about other matters." He smirks.

After all eyes turn to Whitney, she hesitates and says, "Apparently so."

For a moment the room is dead silent.

Whitney notices Fred's eyes fastened on her more than the others. She wonders if he's caught on to her interest in knowing who the young woman, Lynda Ackerman, with the shoes is and her relationship with him.

Charles Whitehead interrupts the silence. "Is that it … are we done?" He looks around at the others to see everyone nod their heads yes. "I guess that does it."

After Whitney leaves Whitehead's office, Whitehead turns to the unknown woman. "Did you profile anything we should know about?"

The unknown woman shakes her head, "Nothing that you don't already know."

Whitehead turns to Rose, "I hope this keeps her quiet. We need to keep this thing low-keyed."

Rose nods his head, yes, "At least she knows we've got tentacles."

Whitehead frowns, "All we need is for her to talk to the media. They'll be all over our asses."

Saunders adds, "To say nothing of the fact that if the public finds out we might as well throw everything out the window. Our reputation to the public and our customers will be zero, if not negative."

Rose lifts his chin ever so slightly, "Let's stop second guessing ourselves. We all agreed on this."

Saunders isn't in full agreement. "What if she goes to the F. B. I.?"

Rose flatly says, "She won't, and you can take that to the bank."

Saunders continues, "Why's that?"

Rose grins, "She doesn't have the balls."

Whitehead puts his hand up, "Let's hope you're right on this."

Rose looks at Saunders, "You got anything else?"

Saunders replies wryly, "No, not at the moment."

Rose nods no as well, "Good."

Saunders' cell phone rings. He looks at it and once he

sees who is calling his face looks angry. "Why the hell is she calling me? I told her I was going to be tied-up in meetings all day!"

Whitehead says, "I'd answer it if I'm right on who it is. It could be important."

Saunders looks at Whitehead, "I know what it's about. She wants me to go with her to a fundraiser tonight, and I don't." Then the cell rings again. He picks up. "Hang on for a second. I have a situation." He listens and then says. "No, I'm not trying to avoid you." He shakes his head in anger. "Just a second, please." He looks at Whitehead and Rose, stands and walks to a corner of the room to continue talking with his wife.

Whitehead says just loud enough for Saunders and Rose to hear, "She's my daughter, so be careful." Then he grins.

Saunders looks at his father-in-law with a hint of disgust, and then with a forced smile and head nod. Then he talks with his wife. "No, I haven't forgotten about tonight." He pauses and then says, "Yes, I'll be there with you. I promise." Another pause and then says, "Love you too." He disconnects and with an angry face turns to the two men listening and watching him. He shrugs his shoulders to put on the best positive outcome he can muster. "There's nothing I wouldn't do for her … my love." He feels his own insincerity. Whitehead and Rose easily pick up on it too, and it isn't hard for them to hide that fact.

CHAPTER 4

The next day Whitney looks at a card with a name and phone number. She makes the call.

"Special Agent McEwen."

She hesitates, reconsidering going through with it. Then she says, "You said if I remembered anything to give you a call."

"That sounds like something I'd say. Who's this?"

"You and your partner Marin … the other night." She hopes McEwen remembers.

"Oh yes, Miss Danica. Yes."

She feels relieved. "I'm not sure what possibly I may know to tell you, but maybe I do and don't yet know it."

McEwen smiles, although Whitney can't see it, "duly noted."

Whitney's brow twitches, and then she glances down at her shoes. "How do we do this?"

"We meet. That's the usual way. Someplace where you'll feel safe."

"My place … tonight at nine."

"Works for me. What's your address?"

"Please, give me some credit. You know where I live." Her eyes widen.

"OK, at nine tonight."

"Come alone." Whitney pauses. "I want protection."

"Do you think your life is in danger?"

"Better safe than sorry."

"I'll see what I can do."

"Oh, one more thing."

"I'm listening."

"I haven't done anything wrong." She catches her breath at the realization she's going to accept protection from the F. B. I. for nothing that she's done but from others who might want her harmed about something she's not sure she knows anything about.

It is 9 pm the same day as Whitney paces in her apartment with a half-glass of Chardonnay in her hand, the third one since she got home. She is nervous and the only thing she thinks about is there are no clean getaways. Still she has a glimmer of hope that she's done the right thing by contacting McEwen. Then something troubling suddenly occurs to her ... maybe she is being set up! She gulps from the wine glass. Who are her friends and what is the truth? The answers to these questions change from second to second as the more she thinks about it, trying to figure out reality, the deeper she sinks into uncertainty. A knock at the front door saves her from thinking more about the predicament. She turns to face the closed door. "Who's there?"

"Me, for our nine o'clock."

Whitney recognizes McEwen's voice but wonders how she got past the downstairs front door without ringing her.

She slowly walks towards the sound and then asks, "How did you get in?"

"Remember who I am. It's not that difficult."

Whitney opens the door with her free hand. The two women face each other as if it is a western gunfight standoff, waiting for the other one to pull out her gun first.

Whitney steps back a few paces, "Come on in." Before closing the door and after McEwen is inside her apartment, she stretches her head into the hallway to look both ways. Then, apparently satisfied that no one is there, she closes the door.

McEwen nods her head, looks at the almost fully drained wine glass and says, "Anything left over? I wouldn't mind."

A brief but important grin flashes across Whitney's face. "It's nice to share." She heads for the small kitchen to pour her guest a full glass while draining the bottle to refill her own.

Returning to the living area, Whitney hands over the glass. "Not to worry … there are more chilled bottles inside the refrigerator." She smiles as she and McEwen in unison take a sip from their own glass.

McEwen nods her head in pleasure. "Napa Region, my guess, but I'm not sure of the vintner. Probably, though, it's production from last year." She looks at the glass of wine in her hand.

"I subscribe to a distribution outfit that automatically sends me a case every once and a while. I can give you their name if you're interested."

"That would be nice."

Then there is silence for a few moments as Whitney takes

a seat followed by McEwen. Both know the pleasantries have been exchanged and it is now down to business.

McEwen starts it off, "Are you scared?"

Whitney lies, "Of what?"

"The unknown."

"The way I see it is there are three of them who think I know something that I don't."

McEwen leans forward, "And that's the unknown. The fact that they THINK you know something is, in this case, more important than what you DON'T know."

"You're sure?"

"I've been doing this for a while. All I'm saying …." She leaves the sentence incomplete on purpose.

Whitney asks, "Are you going to tell me why you're interested in them?" She pauses. Her hand shakes a bit in anticipation of a worse case answer. "It might help me." She takes a sip of wine.

"Help you how?"

"Get over the fact that I AM now freakin' scared!" Her voice is elevated.

McEwen slightly turns her head away and then back to face Whitney. "There are a few things I CAN share, but more that I can't and therefore won't, but more importantly that I can't and won't because this is an ongoing investigation. I'll leave it at that."

"I'll settle for any crumbs … at least for now."

McEwen picks her words carefully to make sure she shares both something and nothing of importance and a few pieces of misleading information. "They are suspected of using foreign money for foreign use in the U.S. … that's illegal, especially when the foreign money is used to influence Federal and State Government decisions on a variety of issues." She pauses, and when she thinks Whitney appears to be sufficiently confused about the something-and-nothing-of-a-sort information, she continues in the same vein. "Influencing Government officials can be very lucrative ... assuming they can get away with it. It isn't easy to prove but it has been in the past and I'm dedicated to make sure it happens here. New owners of a company, like the one you're now working for, have a slight advantage over long established owners of well-known companies since there usually isn't a history of the former company doing anything unlawful as this." She believes she's sufficiently muddied the waters.

"Are you asking me to go undercover?" Her eyes widen, not knowing why she asked the question.

McEwen now knows Whitney has been reeled in. "I'm not asking for anything. Remember who called who?"

Deep in her gut Whitney thinks she knows the truth, but the truth is she has no clue. "But I don't know anything!"

McEwen has been doing this for years, but that doesn't mean it's any easier now. There will be lots more straight out lies and innuendos for Whitney to figure out, which she won't. She knows Whitney will get involved and right now has no idea of the unintended consequences and collateral human damage that will most likely happen. That's just how it is. And once you're in, there's no cutting and running away. She's proud of what she's done with Whitney ... no room for sympathy in her job.

Whitney wets her lips. "I don't want any part of this!" She nervously takes another sip of wine.

McEwen expected this to happen, so she nonchalantly

shrugs her shoulders, stands, and says, "Fine with me. Have it your way. You know how to get a hold of me if you change your mind."

Surprised, Whitney frowns, confused at how easy it was to pull out. Then a sudden realization takes over. "But they saw me with you and your partner!"

"That's what they said. Do you believe them?"

"Why would they say it, if they didn't see it?" Her eyes widen again. "So what am I supposed to do now?"

"It's up to you. It's always been up to you." Her look is intent.

Whitney now thinks that if she wants to live, she's going to have to cooperate with the F. B. I., something new for her. "I've never done anything like this before." Her voice is timid sounding.

"Before you rode a bike, you never rode one before."

"What?"

"What I'm saying is there's always a first time. All you need to do is to do EXACTLY what I tell you to do. No improvising. Always keep me informed. Always be discrete. Don't trust anyone except me. You can count on me to have your back ... always."

Whitney swallows hard. Her throat constricts. She's scared and most likely will be for a longtime ... never feeling really safe ... thinking that she could be tortured and even killed ... they'll be staking out her apartment which, of course, will interfere with her sex life. Sometimes the bad guys act like elephants ... they never forget. Or, maybe she's just being paranoid and that everything will work itself out and be over with shortly.

Whitney takes a deep breath of needed air. "OK, you can count me in."

McEwen picks up her glass of wine, "To us." She holds the glass in the air until Whitney mimics her move and then in unison each takes a sip. "I'd like the name of the distribution company you use."

When Whitney awakes the next morning after meeting with McEwen, she feels differently somehow, not sure if it's a big thing or a small thing, but definitely something. She swings her legs out of bed onto the floor feeling the carpet and the bottoms of her feet meet. For certain, she feels the need for strong coffee ... a solid jolt of caffeine into her veins.

She walks to the bathroom, looks at her face. Her hair is a mess as always the first thing in the morning, but it's her puffy face and noticeable bags under her eyes that make her feel different. Maybe it's a premonition that today is not going to be the best day of her life ... or maybe just the opposite, the best day she's ever experienced!

In one word, she looks SCARED, and she attributes the look and feeling to last night's talk with McEwen. But it was more than a talk, it was a commitment ... something she's cleverly escaped doing with most humans.

She runs her fingers through her messy hair, for a second thinking to keep it that way for today. The customary smell of morning coffee percolating shifts her attention to something more pleasant.

Her next stop is the kitchen for the eagerly anticipated first cup of coffee. She is not disappointed as she notices the automatic coffee machine has dutifully done its job as expected. There is a full carafe waiting for her. She smiles, thankful for a few good things in life that she can count on. The first cup is drunk slowly in order for her palate to savor the flavor, to be exposed to all its ingredients. Her breathing is slow and purposeful, waking up second by second with each inhale of air. Soon, she's onto the second cup that she finishes off much quicker, her taste-buds have already done their job. She sits in one of the two kitchen chairs. "This is nice." She smiles to enjoy the moment, seemingly to have put aside last night's meeting.

Time passes slowly. In an almost dreamlike state she thinks about what last night could have been if her guest was someone other than McEwen ... someone like Jesse. She clearly visualizes him, all alone at her place, each with a drink by their sides.

His soft brown eyes, coal black hair, and his
smile is something she clearly pleasures in.
He leans over towards her to place his warm hand on hers.
She finds herself longing to kiss him.
They kiss for a while and then their temptations
to take it further flow like wine.
She hears him saying, 'I want you now
without any reservations.'
She looks him in the eyes and sees her
reflection with him at their wedding.
Her temptation to go the next step, with his
lips and his hands so sweet is full.
They make love.

Then she suddenly snaps out of the fantasy. It's time for the third and final cup that she pours before getting groomed and dressed for work.

Doing her best to concentrate on work, not on who might be watching her, Whitney stays in her office for most of the day. Then there is a knock on her door that startles her.

She looks up to see Karen standing at the entrance. She smiles at the appearance of a person she can trust.

"I can come back later if now isn't a good time," Karen asks.

Whitney exhales, feeling relieved. "No, no, come in. I need a break right now." She moves to a pair of chairs in front of her desk. As she sits in one, she points to the other, "Have a seat. What's up?"

"I should shut the door." Karen closes the door without a prompt from her boss.

Whitney's smiling look slowly turns to one of worry. "Sure." She swallows.

Karen moves closer to Whitney to take the empty seat. "It's about Lynda Ackerman." Her voice is soft but serious.

Whitney has almost forgotten about her until now. So much seems to be happening at once. "What did you find out?"

"I won't bother you with her academic background and prior job experience. That's all in her résumé and job application form. But what I think is more important is that she and Fred Saunders know each other."

Whitney is now more interested. Her widen eyes tell Karen to continue.

"Family life with our President isn't good. His wife volunteers for every bleeding heart organization and is more than willing to donate financial support without much conversation with her husband. She's a bitch in so many ways, so say people who know her and have worked with her. Then there's their daughter, age 5, who was a surprise to both of them ... unplanned as I've been told. Lisa wants the kid to attend private schools while Fred prefers public. There are religious differences as well between the two."

Whitney interrupts, "What's her name?"

"Lisa. Maiden name is Whitehead." Karen pauses to wait for another question. She sees Whitney's neutral looking face. "Did you already know?"

"Yeah," she nods a few times to support the one word.

"But there's more."

"Go on. Don't let me stop you."

"There are many problems between Fred and Lisa, some of which I've already mentioned. His father-in-law, Charles, is not happy with their situation, and if he could he'd demand they end their marriage immediately, keeping it hush-hush if at all possible. But, he's concerned about image of his family and how it might adversely affect his diverse business interests."

"How does Lynda fit into this?" After hearing her own question, Whitney's face turns in revelation, "no way!"

"Yes, they're having an affair."

"Holy crap!"

"Do you want to know how they met?"

"Honestly no, since there are unlimited ways, but yes, of course, since it's probably just too juicy to keep from me."

"Here's the short version. Lynda was, and still is, involved as a volunteer for a few groups. One of them is a favorite of Lisa's. They took an immediate liking to each other. Then Lisa introduced Lynda to Fred, and voila, that's all it took … timing and motivation. They've been secretly seeing each other for a while … not sure how long, specifically."

"No way!"

"Way!"

"So maybe Fred asked Lynda to check me out, maybe to get some stuff on me that he could use to manipulate me."

"Possible. And here's something else."

"And …."

"To prove to him that she is loyal to him, maybe even implied that a divorce could happen that would lead to marrying him." She wiggles her eyebrows.

"That son-of-a-bitch!"

Later that night, around 11 pm, Whitney's cell phone rings. She snaps out of an unsettled sleep to pick up.

"Whitney!" McEwen's voice on the phone sounds urgent.

Whitney's heart skips a beat, shocked at the late night unexpected call.

"McEwen?" Her voice sounds surprised for sure, but more alarmed for certain.

"Be quiet. Just listen."

Whitney sits up in bed starring within the blackened bedroom.

"Get up now and go to the bathroom. Lock the door and don't come out or say a word until you hear from me again."

"What?" Whitney's mind is foggy and confused.

"Just do it! And do it now!"

Whitney hustles out of bed, bikini panties only, and runs to the bathroom not sure if maybe she's dreaming. She doesn't argue about it, she just does it. She locks the bathroom door.

"McEwen, I'm in." There is no response. Her heart lurches. "Are you there?" Still no response, so she decides to shut down the phone. Then she moves the toilet seat cover down so she can sit. Now shivering with fear in her eyes, she glances around the bathroom, but its darkness is totally making it impossible for her to see anything. She hears nothing except her own deep breathing and her heart beat racing. She swallows deeply, and then randomly moves her hands in the direction of the towel holder which she can't see. Feeling the cotton texture in her hand she pulls it towards her. She wraps the towel around her shivering body. The move helps a bit, but her body's shaking is more related to the panic she feels.

She's sure she is alone in the bathroom, but not the rest of her apartment. She has no way of knowing, although there is a silence all around. Still, she is terrified, waiting for something to happen … to her … by someone.

She tells herself to get a grip by reminding herself that McEwen would have her back … just as she promised … which she reminds herself is right now.

She has no idea what time it is or how long ago the phone woke her up.

She thinks she's thirsty, and needs something to drink. She turns her head to the left while still seated on the toilet seat knowing the sink and faucet are within her reach.

Then she thinks she hears footsteps outside the bathroom, but specifically where inside her apartment is unclear. She catches her breath.

Then, there is a tap, only one, on the bathroom door. "Whitney?"

Under the conditions she isn't sure of the owner of the voice. She remains quiet.

Another tap and then a jingle of the door handle. "Whitney, are you there?"

This time Whitney's almost sure it is McEwen, but how confident can she be under these circumstances? She wants the danger to have passed, but she's not taking any chances, so she stays quiet waiting for something else to confirm her heroine has arrived.

A third tap seals the deal. "It's me, McEwen. All is clear. You can come out now."

Whitney stands, albeit so wobbly that she almost falls, face first, into the wall. She regains her balance, reaches to unlock the door and slowly opens it.

"It's over. Everything is OK." McEwen nods her head and gives Whitney a quick smile.

Whitney stumbles into McEwen's arms.

"Whoa, I've got you." McEwen leads Whitney to the living room area to take a seat.

"What happened?" Whitney's voice is cold as is her almost naked body except for the bikini panties and towel.

"Wait here." McEwen heads for the bedroom thinking there is a robe lying around. Her instincts pay off as she returns to Whitney's shivering side. "Put this on."

The encouragement from McEwen is sufficient for

Whitney to agree, but what she really wants is someone to hold her as tightly as possible.

McEwen thinks the same thoughts but knows better than to provide physical contact … a big no-no. Her voice is formal sounding. "Somebody … we don't know who specifically but I have an idea or two … was on his or her way up. I suspect the intruder was a male but I can't be certain about that since I didn't get a clear look. I don't know how the intruder gained entrance to the lobby floor, so you might want the apartment manager to check into that. The intruder took the stairs and then I suspect got spooked for some reason. I don't know why. Anyway, the intruder got away, and we don't know the motives."

"There's not much that you do know, is there?"

"Not at the present time … affirmative."

"Lucky you were around." Whitney's smile is genuine.

"There'll always be someone close by, whether or not you're in or not. It was by chance that tonight was my rotation."

With that being said, Whitney begins to feel herself again … not totally. How could she? But give it time. At the same time she realizes she'll be under surveillance for quite a while until the situation is resolved, one way or another. But what exactly is the situation? She doesn't know for sure. She stops in mid-thought not wanting to go there. The cold chill from a short time ago returns.

"You're OK now?"

"Yeah, thanks."

"You might put a double lock on the door. Remember ABC … Always Be Cautious."

"Good idea."

"And tell the apartment manager about this. If needed, the manager can give me a call. You've got my number."

"Sure."

With that, McEwen leaves Whitney alone.

CHAPTER 5

After all others have left his office, Whitney stays behind. Fred Saunders looks up wondering why she's still around. "Is there something else?" he casually asks.

"As a matter of fact, there is." As much as she tries to keep a straight face, she grins.

"Is it something that others should know about?"

"That's debatable." Her grin stays put. "But I don't think you'd want that to happen."

Fred, still seated behind his desk places both hands flat on its top, his posture straight and rigid. "Come again?"

"What do you see in her? She's barely out of puberty." Whitney's grin has now turned to a frown of sarcasm flavored with displeasure.

"What are you talking about?" He feels his hands firm up even more.

"Lynda Ackerman." The name is all that is sufficient.

"What the hell are you implying?" He wants to jump over the desk to strangle her.

"Yeah. If you seriously expect me to believe that, you should stop looking like a boy who just lied to his parents about something naughty ... real naughty. It's obvious. And while I'm at it, tell her to tone down her lip movements when

97

she's around you. It's rather embarrassing to say the least. She seems like she'd suck anything, anyone, at any time."

He stands. "I resent your allegations. I could fire you right now and take legal action against you for defamation of character."

She shrugs her shoulders. "Then you should." She stares. "You'll tell your story and I'll tell mine."

He meets her gaze straight on. It strikes him that she is trying to blackmail him. His mind temporarily shuts down but then quickly reboots. "Look, for the record I'm not sleeping with her or anyone else other than my wife, whom I love very much. I have a daughter! But if you're looking for a fight, you'll get one from me!"

"Is that a threat?"

"It's a fact."

She steps forward. "Look, since it's most likely never going to be me now, any time soon, or ever, who you sleep with for whatever reason doesn't concern me … it's strictly your business with whatever consequences result … intentional or unintentional. But I've got to say, tone it down around the office. You and she are currently the main topic of discussion. Don't let your gun manage your affairs. Keep it holstered."

He cocks his head to the side, surprised by her comments. "Thanks for worrying about me." He keeps his gaze squarely in his line of sight, "nothing else?"

"Not at the moment, but I'm sure I'll think of something."

"Then I'm sure you appreciate me asking you to leave me alone so that we both can get back to Company work."

Whitney nods her head, turns, and starts her walk

towards the door. Within a foot from exiting the office she stops, keeps her back to Fred, and says, "The guy you sent to my apartment to intimidate me didn't work. He ran away peeing in his pants." She then leaves his office. No point in pressing any further. She figures he knows what she now does.

Now alone, Fred feels his legs shake and his vision blur up. He lets his body flop into the chair as he thinks about what just happened. He figures he's got a few options. One, ignore it … everything she's said … maybe it's the last of it, which down deep in his psyche he doubts. Two, tell his father-in-law … not likely because the old man would take it personally and find a way to destroy him … so would he if the roles were switched. Three, send out someone who'll handle Whitney once and for all … an accidental fatality. Fourth, offer her a deal she can't refuse …she must want something to keep quiet. Everyone has a price. Why would she bring it up if she wasn't looking for some personal gain? Five, end it with Lynda as painful as it may be. But, what about her reaction … will she get all emotional about ending the relationship and do something really foolish? Six … his mind goes blank for the moment. Hopefully, he'll come up with more possibilities … he doesn't like any of the ones he's already come up with. In the meantime, although temporarily, he's not going to do anything other than shut up.

His phone rings that takes him out of his self-imposed dialogue. "Hello!" His voice is loud and sharp.

"What the hell is going on with you?"

He recognizes his father-in-law's voice, "oh, nothing important. What's up?"

"I just finished reading Whitney's Company Blog Proposal, and honestly, I think it's a work of a genius. I really love it and want to budget it as quickly as possible. Something like this can't wait until the next fiscal year. Have you read it?"

Fred takes a deep breath and slowly lets out the air to calm down. He lies, "Not in its entirety."

"Then you should. It's fantastic. I haven't seen anything as practical and profitable like this in quite a while."

"A game changer, huh."

Charles Whitehead hates the phrase 'game changer' … overused and oversimplified. "Whatever. Just read it. I'll want to seriously talk with you about it."

"OK. Is that it?"

"Are you sure nothing's bothering you that I should know about?"

"No, everything is just fine."

"Well, you don't sound it, but I'll leave that up to you."

"Everything is really fine."

"No problems at home?"

Fred's eyes widen. "Oh no, everything is great."

"You can always come to me to talk things through."

"Yes, I know and I very much appreciate that."

"Fine, after you've read the proposal, let's talk."

The phones disconnect as Fred says to himself, "Chalk up one for Whitney." The more he thinks about it, the more convinced he is that breaking off with Lynda is the right move. Tonight's rendezvous will end it.

As Charles sets the phone on its cradle, his head suddenly snaps to the right. He grabs his head with both hands to steady the involuntary movement. "I'm a sick man. I've got to get this checked out." This is the sixth or seventh consecutive day of lightning bolt flashes from his right eye … he's not sure … he hasn't been counting. He pictures his deceased wife of 27 married years, passed away 5 years ago next month. The mental images of Helen are so vivid that at times they drive him crazy. He often times feels her presence next to him, her smell and her whispering in his ear how much she loves him. He misses his wife very much. Living alone, he concludes, sucks. He is pissed. He wonders if the flashes, him aging, and being alone are somehow connected … probably so but he's not a doctor. He promises to make an appointment with his doctor to assess the flash thing … but he's promised himself that before. Now is the time. It's been going on too long and the more he thinks about it the more concerned he becomes. He doesn't want it to get out of hand. Come to think of it, the new acquisition with all its potential legal issues as well as some probable employee relations problems could be putting an extra strain on him. And come to think of it, he suspects Lisa, his daughter, is having some martial problems with her husband, Fred, the guy he depends upon in running his businesses … just a hunch, but his instincts are usually spot on. He reaches for the phone to make a doctor's appointment.

At a small restaurant that is rarely visited Fred says to Lynda, "We've become emotionally involved in a short time."

Lynda frowns at first and then quickly senses what is about to come next, yet she waits to hear it from him.

Fred drops his eyes to the table top as he continues. "I feel mad at myself for letting something like this happen." He slowly raises his eyes to look at her. "I don't want you to be hurt."

While expected from his opening comment, the reality rocks her back on her heels. Here it is, something she hoped would never happen, but knew down deep in her heart it was simply a matter of time. "Are you simply tired of me?"

He forces a smile that to him is sincere, but to Lynda is as phony as a three dollar bill, "Oh, no, of course not."

"Does Lisa know? Is that it?" She maintains remarkable control of her emotions. "I haven't done anything for her to suspect."

He shakes his head to emphasize, "Definitely not."

"Then why?" She isn't stupid ... she just wants to know why. Is that too much to ask for? "Do you think I'm pregnant?" She pauses, "I'm not."

Under the circumstances, the smart thing to do is to say something ambiguous ... nothing that could come back to haunt him. However it ends, he'll feel differently about many things in the future ... hopefully be a better person, although that's quite doubtful. He's just got to end it quickly. "You're a good person."

She looks at him without blinking. Here it comes, "Yeah."

"The thing is ... I just don't want to see you get hurt."

She knows where this is headed, yet she lies to make him squirm. "I don't know what you really mean?"

"Oh, I think you do. This arrangement can't last forever. You're a super girl with a full life ahead. You're real nice." He knows he's moved into some gibberish.

She takes offense to 'girl' and 'real nice.' "And what the hell does that mean? Has this been just a short term arrangement? And, listen carefully, I'm not a girl, or maybe you haven't noticed!"

He seems to have ignored her comments as he says, "This was never meant to be a quickie thing."

"Quickie!" She tightens her lips. "It's been a year! That's not a quickie arrangement!"

He's still in his own world. "It's just that I can't divorce my wife, so there's no real future for us."

"I've known that all along ... no surprise here. I really like Lisa ... I like being around her. We're friends."

"Don't you want to marry at some point in time?"

While she is frustrated with his line of talk, she gives in. "Not presently, maybe sometime in the future. I don't know." She pauses. "Why do you care?"

"The day is going to come ...."

She interrupts him. "Stop it right now!" She leans towards him, eyes piercing angry. "You're sounding like a parent talking to his daughter! Just stop it! I'm not your daughter! You already have a five year old!"

"Lynda."

"Hey, I get it. It's over and you don't owe me an

explanation, although a reasonable one would have been nice." She nods her head and stands as if she is about to leave, but she stops short. She faces him. "I still want my job." As she walks away, she says, "I'll always remember US together." She turns to face him, "ALWAYS." Then she leaves him alone.

Old sins make long shadows. He knows he can't run away from this sin of adultery, but rather he figures he has to deal with it or it will just get bigger to cast a longer shadow as time passes. In other words, if he doesn't do something this sin will haunt him forever.

He rubs the nape of his neck and rolls back his head. He hears vertebrae cracking, and then feels a little relief, yet he knows the reprieve will be short lived.

CHAPTER 6

Whitney is not sure where she comes from, more specifically who her parents are, whether she really lived with her biological mother and father or someone else. Yet in her gut she's always been suspicious that people lied to her, keeping from her many things ... everyone has shadows ... baggage, hidden agenda, thin skins, passive-aggressive tendencies, self-interest, secrets, and so on ... the list is endless. And she knows she's no different than the rest.

She does remember having an unusual high level of fantasy ... making up people she never met ... places that she never visited or for that matter even existed ... situations that she simply composed out of thin air ... a language that only her and her make believe friends understood. At first, people such as teachers and classmates found it entertaining, but as she got older they grew leery of her emotional mental state, especially as it pertained to the real world. At those times, others would stare at her in frustration and confusion ... some even were afraid of her.

Today she wonders about her origin albeit less so now than then. Still, at times of emotional mental distress she thinks about what she so desperately wants to know, but can't. And the odds of finding out about her past are slim to none, so she sets aside those thoughts, but obviously not entirely. She knows she'll return to them again, but when, she's not sure. It's anybody's guess.

She lies still in bed when the nearby cellphone rings on the night stand next to her bed. It is six in the morning. She opens her eyes, reaches for the cell phone, peers at the white popcorn ceiling to wait for the second and third rings that will trigger her seven second greeting, a single beep, and then the incoming message. She listens to the sound of the caller, and then catches her breath at the surprise … it's her former husband who walked out on her to be with his male lover! "Whit, I miss you. I wanna get back together."

Sometimes, when something is so painful to deal with, you invent reasons for what happened. You see, it's much easier to imagine than to deal with reality because the cosmos is composed of random hits and misses. Sometimes you choose between what you feel and what you think, although for many that distinction is often difficult to tell the difference. What this means is we make mistakes, but it is those mistakes that are our best teachers.

She flashes back to her childhood and feels the sense of isolation she felt then. Where does she come from … who is betraying her and why … or is she simply shocked over the unexpected phone call?

Soon after he left her, she was mad as hell. Then, for some reason, she began to think he'd return to her quickly, apologize for his stupid behavior, and everything would be hunky-dory. But that didn't happen, which left her with only one reasonable alternative … she really didn't give a damn about him anymore. So, in the end he drifted away from her like a stream of smoke.

She shuts down the cell phone, replaces it on the night stand, turns her body away, and closes her eyes to get a few more minutes of sleep.

The same morning Charles is at his doctor's office. The eye exam, blood pressure, weight, a discussion of his diet and exercise routine is completed by a competent medical clinician. She types into his record the results that immediately are transferred to Doctor Beckson's computer.

"OK now," Diana Snyder says, "the last part is to dilate your eyes. This is easy and it's like eye drops, so keep still and keep your eyes wide open." She finishes the procedure within seconds and hands him a tissue. "Excellent work, here's a tissue if you need to wipe your cheeks from any dripping of the fluid. Now, let me take you to Doctor Beckson who'll examine your eyes.

Forty minutes later Charles sits across from Doctor Beckson, his private physician, who has completed several steps in exploring the condition of each eye. Finally, he sits down on a stool in front of Charles who remains seated in the patient's chair. "Charles, there's nothing to worry about."

Charles feels very relieved and manages to put forth a big smile. His body loosens up. "That's good news. I was worried, and honestly, was expecting the worse." He pauses, and then asks, "Is there a sandwich in your feedback?" His face has returned to being solemn.

Beckson hesitates to think about the analogy, and once

he makes sense of it he says, "No, it's not good news at both ends with the bad news in between." He touches Charles' right knee for assurance. "Let me tell you what's going on."

Charles nods his head to proceed.

"The back of the eye is filled with a clear gel similar to egg white. The gel is called vitreous. As a person ages, the vitreous changes naturally … it's a normal part of the aging process … nothing unusual. What it does is it liquefies and shrinks. And this natural process may cause the symptoms you've been having … flashing lights and even floating spots in the field of vision. Have you seen these floaters as well?"

"Come to think of it, yes."

Beckson nods his head. "Of course, it's natural. Most of the time this is normal and nothing to worry about, but sometimes it can cause something potentially serious with the retina, which is the part of the eyes that is the source of vision."

"Is this the bad news part?"

"Not for you. You're OK." Beckson smiles and continues. "Floaters are those shadows of tiny bits of protein floating in the clear gel. When you move your eye, these floaters sway back and forth across your vision. They can look like strings, lines, dots, and so forth. They can be small or large, and are most frequently noticed when you look at a blank wall or the blue sky."

"Yes, I can relate," Charles agrees.

"Sometimes the gel tugs on the inner eye wall as it begins to shrink. This tugging may cause split-second flashes of light, especially when the eye or head is moved suddenly."

Charles adds, "Like from a camera flash or a lightning bolt."

"Exactly," Beckman nods his head, delighted his patient is following the explanation. "And these flashes are usually near the edge of your vision and more obvious to you in the darkness." He pauses, "So far, so good?"

Charles nods his head, yes, without comment.

Beckson continues. "Flashes and floaters are obvious distractions, but they are not usually dangerous. In most cases, like the ones you're experiencing, they become less bothersome and eventually will stop … but not all the time for everyone. For a few people they can result in a hole or tear in the retina, a serious problem that could lead to vision loss if not detected and treated. You have nothing to worry about. There is no tear, no blood, no evidence of a hole, or anything else I could find from examining you."

"So I'm good to go?"

"Yes, but one more thing."

Charles wonders if this is the bad news … saving the worse to last. He takes in a deep breath as his body stiffens.

Beckson notices Charles's stiffening body. "This is all good, don't worry." He taps Charles' knee once again for assurance. "When a patient has flashes and floaters but no retinal tear or hole, there is no treatment needed."

"No diet, exercise, vitamins and so forth?"

"You always want to eat healthy, exercise, take appropriate vitamin supplements, and do other steps to drop your blood pressure, but that's for everyone. There are no eye-drops, vitamins, glasses, exercises, and so forth to make them go away. It may take weeks, months, or even years for them to disappear. You are not in any danger with respect to the flashes and floaters. There is no need for a follow up appointment."

Charles blinks quickly a few times, still a little nervous over the whole thing.

"Here's what to look out for ... an increase in the flashes and floaters, or a sudden partial or full loss of your side vision. If any of these symptoms occur, call us for a follow-up appointment."

"You're the Doctor." Charles pauses and then continues his thought. "It's better than the ultimate alternative."

"And what's that?"

"A little discomfort with age is better than not aging at all." The sound of his voice is more of relief than a joke.

There is a split second of silence and then a simultaneous laugh from both men.

"Anything else you want to talk about?"

Charles smiles, feeling good about the news. He hesitates before moving onto another subject, not sure why he's thinking about it. He decides to talk. "You know my records. Mostly good health but had a stroke a few years back that required serious intervention. My wife, Helen, was still living then." He abruptly stops talking, blinks his eyes a few times and coughs. He's upset just thinking of her.

"You don't have to go on."

"No, I'm OK. This has been bugging me for quite a while and now's just as good of a time to get it off my chest." He smiles to Beckson. "This is not about my eyes, but something else."

"Sure, go on. I'm listening." Beckson nods, curious of what's on his patient's mind. "You're in safe hands." His face is peaceful looking.

Charles gazes towards the back of the small room, his eyes just about at Beckson's shoulders. "It's all in my records.

Well not everything, just the surgery part." He swallows and then continues. "I was hospitalized ... on a waiting list for a heart transplant ... one out of a million odds, at least." He grins. "Anyway this boy about 17 years old was killed ... a freak motorcycle accident ... killed him instantly ... really a bad situation." He shakes his head weightily. "If I were his parent I'm not sure I'd know how to handle it." His face looks sad and sorrowful. "Then a day later, call it the arrangement of the stars in the heavens, I don't know what to call it, his heart and my heart were matches. Bingo! I was going to be the recipient of a new heart! Unbelievable!" He wipes his mouth with the back of his hand. "I was amazed, the doctors were amazed, and so was Helen. We couldn't believe it." His face shines with joy. "Anyway the operation was a total success. I wanted to thank the kid's parents, but as you probably know that connection is usually denied unless the donor's family agrees, which is not often. At any rate I began feeling 20 years younger, at least. I started to listen to music that I had enjoyed when I was younger. I bought clothes that were more suitable for someone much younger than me, and my appetite for food and wine grew. I thought my taste buds had been replaced! Sounds all so good ... doesn't it." He looks at the doctor.

Beckson shrugs his shoulders, still intrigued by the story and his patient's clear remembrance of it all, but is not sure what medical advice he can offer ... maybe just to listen is enough.

Charles continues. "Helen started to get annoyed with my changes. I tried to talk with her about it but she was too stubborn for a heart-to-heart. I think she was becoming jealous of the new-me." His expression is deadpan for a few seconds. "I think I was beginning to feel like the kid whose heart was now beating inside me. Is that crazy or what?"

Beckson clears his throat. "I guess that's possible." Nothing else comes to mind to say.

"I think Helen was thinking that I was getting closer to the kid and further away from her. That's what I began to think." He looks away for a split second but hurries back to continue. His voice is now pumped with enthusiasm. "And then another strange thing happened … it took both Helen and me by surprise. You wanna know?"

"Of course, keep on talking." He nods his head up and down.

"The kid's family, through the Hospital, contacted me to say they wanted to meet me! Can you believe that?" He's not looking for a response from Beckson, so he quickly continues. "Wow! So I said fine, but Helen wanted no part of it. I pleaded with her but she still refused. She told me to meet them alone." He takes in a deep breath of air, lets it out slowly, and resumes. "I met the parents, very nice couple who seemed sincerely interested in knowing about me, the recipient of their son's heart. They were great … kind, caring, and compassionate, a real class act. When I got back home I couldn't wait to share this with Helen, but she wanted no part of it. So, I told myself never to bring up the subject again. But secretly, that family and me got to become real close, yeah." His voice softens as he stares at the wall right behind Beckson. "Then Helen passed on and it seemed at the same time I lost interest in keeping the relationship with them. Every time they called the house, I told them I was busy with something." He shakes his head sideways just a little and folds his hands one over the other.

Beckson wonders if it's his turn to say something. "Thanks for sharing that."

"Yeah, at least I feel better. Thanks for listening. I guess we all need someone to listen to us. Yeah, I think we all do."

Charles arrives later than usual at work due to the ophthalmology appointment. He does his best to be in high spirits, but he figures that'll take a little time. Otherwise, he considers life to be reasonably good. However, it all changes when he steps into his office.

Fred Saunders and Hank Rose sit alongside each other on the couch, faces are nervous. Charles immediately forgets what he had just said to himself. It seems to him that the wolves have come out to scare his partners. He doesn't have time to ask a question.

Rose says, "Did you read this morning's paper?" His high pitched voice even frightens him. He raises the paper in his hand.

"Not yet, I was at a doctor's appointment. What's so important?"

Fred's voice is urgent, concerned about what might happen next. "It's on the front page! Everyone is going to read it! We're done!" He stands paralyzed with unexpected intensity as his eyes go wide. Then he almost falls over with fright.

Some people try to negotiate reality, creating a self-truth that satisfies them, but the comfort lasts for a very short time. Charles knows there's danger. "Talk to me. What does it say?"

Hank answers. His voice is now moderated a bit from

just before. "Essentially it says our Company is snake oil. That we rip off distressed companies by buying them at a near to a ground-level price, reduce them to almost nothing by cutting expenses, and then resell them quickly for a profit." His stare is from an almost totally pale face.

Charles listens to what is said and then looks down at his feet. He shakes his head in irritation. "Who the hell has been talking to the press?" He lifts his head to face both men. "There's a blabbermouth, a snitch in our midst. Who the hell is it? Who's betraying us?"

Hank steps forward, "It can't be our inner team. It's got to be someone new."

Fred adds, "Someone from the Company we just bought."

For a short time there is dead silence. Not even their own breathing is heard. Then Charles makes a point. "Our biggest problem isn't from within. It's from outside." He looks at the two men whose faces show confusion. "It's the F. B. I., it has to be." He strokes his head, impatient as well as nervous, wondering how the F. B. I. could possible know their secrets ... any of them. He is troubled.

Hank's head barely shakes sideways to offer another insight. "Sure, the F. B. I. is our problem, but someone had to inform the press. And that person or persons had to be insiders. There's no other way to explain it. I'm convinced this was started by an insider. No doubt in my mind."

"So, what do you propose?" Charles slips behind his desk.

Hank answers. His voice is confident. "Eliminate the impossible and whatever remains is the possible. Within the possible is the probable, and that is where you'll find the truth."

Fred shows a little grin, "OK, Sherlock."

Hank turns to face Fred. "It's the only logical way to find out who started this." He pauses. His face now shows a bit of a smirk. "Do you have another idea, Dr. Watson?"

Fred says, "I'm pretty sure I know who did this but I can't prove a thing." He figures this is his chance to get rid of Whitney.

Hank says, "Knowing is good."

Fred replies, "Proving it is better."

Charles shows exasperation. "What the hell are you two talking about?"

Fred turns to his father-in-law and in a calm voice he says, "I'm pretty sure it's Whitney."

Charles' spontaneous and involuntary surprise lasts for a fraction of a second. His jaw drops but his mouth remains shut. Momentarily his eyebrows rise. "What?"

Fred quickly turns towards Hank and then back to Charles. "I didn't trust her the first time I met her and now, having had a few meetings with her, I'm convinced she's not onboard. She's out for herself."

Charles is still stunned. "Have you read her Company Blog Proposal?"

"Not fully."

"Then you ought to. It's outstanding as if she is some sort of whiz kid." Charles turns to Hank, "Did you read it?"

Hank nods his head affirmatively. "Yes, and I agree it is an outstanding Proposal, something, quite honestly, I would never have thought of. She's sure got talent."

Charles looks at Fred, "See." He pauses to think about

something and then continues. "What else is going on that I should know about?"

Fred is now the one who's surprised, but probably more shaken by the question. "What do you mean?"

Since the first attempt failed, Charles tries another way of making his point clear. "You are not acting rationally. Something personal is happening in your life that is clouding your thinking. I don't know what it is, who it is, or why it is, but IT IS, and it's got to stop. Find a way to solve whatever it is because it's interfering with your work here. Maybe you need to take some time off. We've all been putting in incredible hours making this deal happen, and we've still got an enormous amount of work to do before we sell the Company at a profit. I can't have one of the key players disabled in any way." His intent look emphasizes his point. "Am I clear?"

Fred opens his mouth, "I …." His head bows as if he was back in high school, just admonished by his 9th grade English teacher, Miss Little, for something he purposely did that he knew he shouldn't have done but did it anyway. He nods with his head still tilted downward. His voice is soft, almost a hush that is barely heard, "Yes."

CHAPTER 7

Mid-morning the next day in Whitney's office she and Karen talk about the Company Blog Project. "My hunch tells me we're going to get funded. And with you, as the Project Manager, will be a star. I'm convinced of it."

Karen's eyes sparkle in joy. She feels like jumping up and down as would a child with a surprise gift. "I can't believe this."

"It's not official. It's just my hunch." Whitney shares Karen's happiness. "In anticipation of the approval and eventual funding, you should start thinking about building a team of people you believe in and trust, who'll focus and focus and then focus some more. Anybody come to mind?"

Karen rolls her head to the side to loosen up muscles that seem to tighten. "This might sound weird, but I really think that Lynda Ackerman has the right skill set. I've seen her work and she's good ... very good."

Whitney's lips protrude and her eyebrows are raised, "Seriously?"

Karen nods her head affirmatively. "I know what you're thinking."

Whitney casts a glance away from Karen, lifting her face ever so slightly, and then returns to face her again. A grin

117

cuts across her face. "What better way to keep an eye on her than to have her working closely with you." She chuckles. "I love it ... who else?"

"There's Josh, Cindy, Phyllis, and Daryl. They're all excellent and I've teamed up with them before on other projects."

"OK, that's enough for now. Let's do this. Talk with Lynda first. See how she responds to you ... but no commitment yet. Then come back to me to talk further."

"I'm on it right away."

Karen walks towards Lynda's workstation but finds the area vacant. She calls out to Josh, "Have you seen Lynda today?"

"No ... I don't think she's come in yet."

"Has she called in?"

"Not to my knowledge. Maybe she talked with H. R.?"

Karen knocks on the office of H. R. before entering. She sees Sheldon Samuelson sitting behind his desk with heaps of paper scattered everywhere. "Sorry to bother you, but just a quick question." She steps inside the office.

Sheldon looks up. His face suggests he is in low spirts. The corners of his mouth are depressed and his eyebrows are raised. He says nothing.

"Has Lynda Ackerman called in sick today?"

Sheldon seems relieved with the seemingly bland question. It could have been worse. He clears his throat.

"No, not that I'm aware of ... have you checked with her supervisor?"

"I don't think she's been assigned one ... remember the, uh, new reorganization eliminated most of those positions. Most everyone now is self-directed. I knew it wouldn't work." She lets out a puff of air in disapproval of the new set up.

"Give it time. That's how the new owners want it." Sheldon is eager for Karen to leave him alone. Beneath his desk his right leg starts jumping up and down.

"Can you give her a call?"

Now it's Sheldon's turn to let out a puff of air in disapproval. "Sure ... sure."

She knows he's lying, and she knows that he knows that she knows he's lying. She shakes her head sideways and then turns half way around. "I'd appreciate it if you'd let me know what you find out." She walks away.

"Lynda's not at work. Nobody seems to know where she is ... I asked Josh. Then I went to H. R. who was of no use. Sheldon said he'd call Lynda and get back to me, but I don't believe him. He's useless." Karen's body slightly sways in a slight tremble ... she is upset as she stands in Whitney's office.

"I know how you feel. We'll work around it." Whitney feels the same frustration. "Do you have her cell number ... do you know where she lives?"

"I can find out. Why?"

"Make a call. If there's no answer, go visit her."

Karen shrugs her shoulders at what seems to be an obvious solution. "Sure, I'll do that now."

An hour later, Karen stands outside Lynda's apartment building. Her call into Lynda a short time ago went unanswered. The building is new and located in a part of town where the rents are pricey. It is one of the toniest buildings in town. She wonders how someone like Lynda can afford the classy place with the salary she's making at WRS. Maybe her parents are footing the bill … maybe she has a second job … maybe she knows somebody. Karen doesn't really know and at the present time puts aside in finding out. That's none of her business.

She approaches the front door that she assumes will be locked. She's not surprised when she tries to pull open the door. She looks around wondering what next to do when unexpectedly a U.S.P.S. delivery worker walks to the rear of the building with a package in his hand. Something comes to mind, so she follows him.

Now at the rear of the building she sees a sign, **_Deliveries_**. The worker fumbles with the package while trying to push a button to gain access. This is Karen's opportunity. She calls out, "Hey, let me help you."

The worker turns his head towards her, "Hey, thanks."

"Is that for me? I'm Lynda Ackerman, unit 1010. I'm expecting something important."

He looks at the mailing address, "No, not yours. Sorry."

"Whatever."

They jointly walk into the building together but at the first opportunity she sees, Karen veers away from him to find the stairways toward the tenth floor. She feels her heart beat pick up as she presses forward with each step she takes. She's never done anything like this before, but she admits to herself that it feels exhilarating. Quickly, however, she slows down, realizing her lack of physical conditioning. At the fifth floor, she stops to rest a minute, and then continues until she reaches the tenth floor for one last break.

Apartment 1010 is at the far end of the hallway, away from the elevator where it is the quietest. She stands in front of the apartment door and then knocks twice. There is no answer, so she tries again, but this time calls out, "Lynda, are you there?" but the result is the same. She reaches towards the door handle and is surprised when the door easily opens with her first try. She steps inside the apartment, "Lynda, are you there?" Again, there is no response.

Slowly she closes the door to look around. She remains standing just inside the door entrance. The first thing that catches her attention is the striking view of the City through a large window. There is an opened bottle of wine with two empty glasses on a table. She notices a wine opener nearby. There are artsy looking paintings on the wall. The place is clean and tidy, with an antiseptic feel to it.

She walks around, first reaching the bedroom. The bed is unmade. There are ample clothes in the closet. The bedroom walls are wall papered with an exotic design that Karen doesn't recognize.

She moves to the bathroom that is orderly looking.

Now in the kitchen, she opens the refrigerator that is mostly empty with only a few cartons of uneaten takeout food. There is not a dish in the sink or in the dishwasher. All dishes, cups, saucers, pots and pans, and utensils are appropriately stored in cabinets or drawers. There is no coffee maker.

Now, back in the main living room, Karen takes a final head turn. She doesn't know what to conclude other than Lynda is not present and whoever she was waiting for to have drinks with either didn't arrive or something bad happened. She feels nervous and now wants to leave quickly to tell Whitney what she's seen. The exhilarating feeling has been replaced with fear.

"Did you touch anything?" Whitney conceals her heightened nervous emotion.

"I – I don't think so." Karen is not able to cover up her fear. "But – but I had to open the door, so I did touch the door handle, and the same with the refrigerator, dishwasher ... uh ... cabinets and drawers."

Whitney blinks a few times. "Don't worry. You didn't do anything wrong." Her voice is calm but she feels her stomach churn inside.

"I – I broke into her apartment!" Her wild-looking eyes show stress and fright. "Do we call the police?"

"No to both. You didn't break in. You said the door was open and you said you were helping the postal worker."

"Come on, that's semantics."

Whitney ignores the challenge. "And no, we don't call the police. Did you sense any kind of struggle?"

"I don't know ... I'm not a cop ... I don't know what that would look like!"

"So, this is just between us. Don't tell anyone, and I do mean no one." Whitney eyes squint, "Let's see what H. R.

does. Sheldon said he'd call Lynda later today." Privately, she quickly concludes that Fred is behind Lynda's disappearance, and decides to keep her thoughts private for now. "If Lynda doesn't show for work during the next few days, H. R. will have to do something, maybe even go to her apartment with or without the police. But, and here's something I don't know for sure, if no one other than H. R. reports Lynda is missing from work, will the police investigate? They might just think that Lynda simply took off for a few days ... no big deal. But, I really don't know that answer."

Special Agent Paula McEwen talks with her partner, Special Agent Scott Marin. "Whitehead, Rose, and Saunders have a long record. They've made many behind-the-scene deals that placed many people in important Government positions, both Federal and State, most of whom were not even remotely qualified to do the job, but were grateful and indebted to them. They have influenced appointing staffers for Attorney Generals, Judges, and Administrators for several Agencies. Bribes and other illegal payments have been common to buy favors that advanced their businesses, and now our investigation shows that they are working on putting someone they've bought into a big political appointment at the Federal level right now. They find ways to give everyone something, and they keep most people in the dark, sharing as little detail as possible ... less is better than more. Up to now, rumors about them were constant, a way of life, but now we've got more than rumors. Prostitution is common, paying girls and boys up to five grand for an hour of entertainment." She shakes her head in disgust but moves on. "Of the three, Fred Saunders is the most active, yet he is naïve and narcissistic enough not to worry as much as he should. He's like a panting dog in heat. His father-in-law, Charles Whitehead, tries to keep him on a tight leash, especially since he is married to his daughter, and he and his wife have a five year old daughter. But this guy's addicted. He's humping one of the employees, Lynda Ackerman" She pauses. "And their Chief Legal Counsel, Hank Rose, is, and I hate to admit it, but he's very, very good." She pauses again.

Marin asks a question, "But can we trust Danica? How do we know she won't turn on us, especially if they give her something she can't turn down?"

"Great question, I don't know, to be honest. I really don't know."

One day later, a young woman is found dead in a dumpster in a nearby alley from Lynda's apartment. A homeless person literally fell over her when he was scrounging around for food. The police think she might have been strangled since there were marks on her neck. She was fully clothed which implied no sexual assault. She was wearing tight fitting jeans, a blouse without a bra, and shoes but without socks. She might have been tortured since her pink skin suggested lividity … that is when the blood settles into the skin's capillaries as they dilate after circulation ceases, resulting in a purple discoloration but pinkish when the body is in a cold environment. There was a small tattoo of a black rose on her left ankle. Her name, if known, was not released immediately.

It's quite unusual when two or more people witness something at the same time that they see it the same way. And as time moves forward, these same people even remember something different than what they first observed. Maybe it's because each of us has a unique point of view, and, in a way biased. So, go figure, but it happens, and it probably has happened to you.

Medical examiners look at a dead body to figure out the reason for the fatality, while law enforcement look at the same dead body for clues on how to find the culprit. No one really knows for sure how the dead woman spent her final time right before her death.

McEwen says to Marin, "The police have identified the deceased woman as Lynda Ackerman. They found a photo I.D. in her pants pocket. We know she was intimate with Fred Saunders. Maybe she was going to break it off with him ... to move onto greener pastures." She shrugs her shoulders.

Marin shakes his head in disagreement. "Here's how I see it." He waves his hands to help explain his theory although there isn't anything symbolic about his hand movement. "He's the one who was going to call it quits ... getting too cozy for him, especially since his boss is his father-in-law. I can't believe Charles Whitehead would take kindly in knowing that his son-in-law was sleeping around."

McEwen puckers his lips, "OK, let's go with that." She pauses, "Therefore she was going to plead with him to give it a little longer, to convince him to hang in there ... that's why there was an opened bottle of wine. She knew she had a sweet deal."

Marin nods to agree, "But something must have set him off."

McEwen looks upward at nothing specific, "Assuming there wasn't someone else with her, not him."

Marin nods, "There could have been Saunders and another man, maybe a woman. You see what I'm getting at." His pause to collect his thoughts lasts too long.

McEwen exclaims, "She was having multiple affairs with men and women!"

Up to this point Detective Burns from the City's Police Department has been quiet. Now it is his time to add his thoughts. "Hold on, your imagination has taken over your critical thinking. Bring it back to reality."

Marin defends his and McEwen's resourcefulness. "At this point in the investigation, nothing is too farfetched."

Burns asks, "Why is the F. B. I. so interested in this case? So far, I haven't heard anything that would lead me to believe it's anything more than a local murder. Or haven't you told me everything."

Marin looks at McEwen who explains. "There are three players we've been following for a few years. That would be Charles Whitehead, Fred Saunders, and Hank Rose. They've been working one kind of scheme or another for quite a while, and then they crossed over from local stuff to … let me just say global stuff."

Burns twists his nose, "Like what?"

McEwen looks at Marin and then back at Burns. "This is between us, OK?"

Burns nods his head in agreement, "OK, I'm listening."

"We suspect these three hoods have been directly involved in money laundering, interference of U.S. Government appointments at various levels and in various agencies, wiretapping, and computer hacking, just to name a few. They've even been participants in drug trafficking and accessory to prostitution. They buy companies who need an infusion of immediate cash to keep functioning, and then they strip them blind to resell them at a profit. We've got bits and pieces of a lot of things but nothing yet that we feel is solid evidence for an arrest. If Saunders was responsible for the woman's death, then we feel that would be sufficient to charge him, and then, well, we hope he'd want to cut a deal."

Marin adds, "He'd betray his closest friend or family member to save his own hide."

Burns nods his head a few times, "But you really don't know who killed her. It doesn't seem anywhere close to a suicide, so that's been ruled out."

"We're working on it," Marin says. His voice is a mixture of defiance and regret.

Burns pushes on. "The Feds have far more rules than I do at the local level. Let me handle the case. I might be able to do things you can't." He wiggles his eyebrows a few times.

McEwen and Marin look at each other with a hint of favorable reception of the idea. Then McEwen turns to Burns, "Let me think about it."

Burns senses the opening. "I can get to Saunders more easily than you. You're obvious, I'm not."

Marin says to McEwen, "And maybe Danica as well."

The next day, after hearing from McEwen, Burns meets

with Saunders in a nearby café against the strong advice from both Rose and his father-in-law who both believe Saunders should have legal representation present during the meeting.

Burns starts it off. "Thanks for meeting with me."

"No problem. What's this about?"

"One of your employees ... I should say former employee."

Saunders' brow knits. "Former, is that what you said?"

"Yeah."

"Who?"

"Lynda Ackerman."

Saunders' eyes open as wide as a light bulb.

"You do know Lynda Ackerman ... don't you." Burns is interested in keeping the conversation personal, not dehumanizing it in any way.

"Well, we, ugh, just bought the Company, so I'm not aware of all their names."

"How long ago was that?"

"What?"

"When you bought the Company, how long ago?"

"Uh, I'd say, uh, maybe a few months, more or less."

He tries to confuse Saunders. "Are you sure, maybe a year more or less?"

Saunders takes in a deep breath, "no way." Saunders swallows and then continues. "What about her, the employee?"

"Lynda Ackerman is dead." Burns' voice is a matter of fact, without emotion.

Saunders can't look Burns in the eyes. He turns away, "Oh my God!" He forces his eyes shut as he rethinks if his decision to meet alone with Burns was a good idea. Maybe he should have followed the advice from Rose and his father-in-law. It's too late now.

"I'm sorry to be the first one to tell you." Burns surveys Saunders who touches his ear, like a 'tell' during a poker game. He wonders how truthful Saunders is.

"I don't know what to say." Saunders puts his hand over his face.

Burns recognizes the move as a stalling tactic, so he waits him out.

Saunders continues, now having come up with what he hopes is a convincing response. "I'm sorry to hear. Has her family been notified?"

Burns watches him swallow, surprised in a way that the man sitting across from him is so obvious. He'd been led to believe by the F. B. I. that this guy was shrewd. "Did you know Lynda Ackerman well?"

"Who … the girl?"

"Yeah, that's who we're talking about, Lynda Ackerman." Burns recognizes the repeat question as another stalling tactic, so he keeps quiet.

Then Saunders says in a hurried fashion, "Wait a minute. Let me get this straight … you're seriously asking me …." He lets his voice trail off.

"What do you think I'm asking you?" Burns tilts his head to the side.

It comes out of Saunders' mouth too quickly to retract. "I haven't been unfaithful to my wife for all the years we've been married. Hell, we've got a young daughter!"

Burns keeps his grin to himself. He thinks it's incredible

that the man is so stupid so he pushes on, "Just the past ... what ... few months, years ... what?"

Saunders wipes his nose with the back of his hand realizing he's played the wrong card. He fumbles for an answer. He lies, "Something like that ... not long."

"How did it start with Lynda?" Burns' eyes are unblinking.

He knows he's been caught in a lie. "It was her who was interested in me in starting the relationship. Not me."

"That's interesting." Burns' leans back in his chair.

"I didn't set out to get into this mess. She called me."

"Oh man, how these broads know how to work their mojo on us. They can be ruthless." Burns puts on a compelling grin.

"Tell me about it." Saunders shakes his head sideways in defeat as he swallows.

"So it was Lynda's fault. Is that what you're saying?"

"No, no, I'm not blaming her. I didn't have to meet with her secretly, but I did. She was interested in the same things I was." His voice sounds pathetic as if he is trying to cover up something about her.

"Was Lynda seeing another man?"

"I don't know. How could I? I never asked."

"Did Lynda like women, too?"

"What are you saying?"

"I'm not saying anything. I'm asking a question. You know what I'm asking. Just answer."

"I don't know." His voice is somber.

"When was the first time you and Lynda did the deed?"

"What kind of question is that?"

"An important one ... just answer it."

Saunders looks away as if he is embarrassed to answer or perhaps just trying to concentrate on the answer ... the appropriate one based on the situation he's in. "I don't remember."

"When was the last time you saw Lynda Ackerman?"

"A few days ago."

"Do you mean two days, maybe three or four? Be specific."

"I don't remember."

"Where specifically ... in the office, at a restaurant, at a hotel, or just maybe her place?"

"At Lorenzo's."

"What's that?"

"A small Italian restaurant, nothing special."

"What happened there?"

"What do you mean, what happened?"

"What did you and Lynda talk about ... what did you do ... you know ... that sort of thing?"

"I told her we had to stop seeing each other."

"So, it was you who broke it off?"

"Yeah, it was me."

"Not Lynda?"

"No, I said it was me."

"OK, if you say so. Why?"

"It should have never happened. I guess I was feeling guilty." Saunders is now is in his element, the environment of lying.

"Why did it take you so much time to come to that conclusion? Were you ready to move onto someone else?"

"Who the hell do you think you're talking to?" Saunders leans over the table in defiance.

Burns is undeterred. "Don't play the 'I'm offended card' with me. Just answer the question." He remains unfazed with it all.

"It was the right thing to do." He pinches his lips tightly together. "I realized it was wrong."

"How did Lynda take it?"

Saunders seems to have settled himself down, "Remarkably well."

"Did that surprise you?"

"At first, yes, but after I thought about it, I thought about something else."

"What was that?"

Saunders' clears his throat. "The last thing she said to me was that she would ALWAYS remember our time together. She emphasized ALWAYS."

"And that meant what to you?"

"That she had the intention to blackmail me."

"Thus, you had motive to kill Lynda."

"That's preposterous. I would never do that, never, so help me God."

"Not only motive, but if you had access to the apartment that it seems you paid for, you had a key, which means opportunity."

"Who said I paid for her apartment? Huh? That's absurd!" He pauses to collect his thoughts and to calm down. "I swear on my mother's grave, I did not kill her." His lips quiver and he makes a sudden jerky facial move. "I swear it."

"Who else knew about your affair with Lynda Ackerman?"

"Whitney Danica." He's definitely not going to let his father-in-law or Rose know the details of this conversation.

Later the same day, Burns calls McEwen. "I've got an update, if you're interested."

McEwen motions to Marin to move closer. "I'm putting you on speaker. I want Agent Marin to hear this. Go on, we're listening."

"It's my opinion that Saunders didn't kill Ackerman. He might have had motive and opportunity, but he just doesn't seem to be the type."

"And what type is that?"

"It's just my instincts. He's not the one."

Marin asks, "I'm missing something here. He had everything to gain by making her disappear for good, and as much to lose if she yakked about it. There isn't anyone else as I see it." He glances at McEwen who nods in agreement.

McEwen has the same opinion. "That's how I see it too."

Burns differs. "I'm not going to bring a charge against him without real evidence. Maybe that's how the Bureau does it, but I'm not going to do it."

While hesitant, McEwen falls in line with him. "So, for discussion sake, what's your next move, if you count Saunders out of the equation?"

Burns clears his throat. "When I asked him who else might know about the affair, he gave me a name."

McEwen smacks her lips, "Who?"

"Somebody named Whitney Danica."

McEwen and Marin look at each other in surprise

as their eyes momentarily widen and then draw back to normal. Silence slices through the phone conversation.

Burns asks, "Does the name ring a bell with either of you?"

McEwen nods her head, but keeps the tone of her voice more casual to be careful of not sharing too much information at the present time, although that soon becomes difficult to continue, "Oh, yeah. We know her. She's someone who's giving Whitehead, Saunders, and Rose a hard time. I don't think there's any chance of them developing a constructive relationship with her."

"Tell me more."

"She's an employee at the senior level who has been the victim of a near fatal poisoning, and an apartment break-in."

Burns asks, "Any connection between them and the two incidences?"

"Nothing we can prove."

Marin adds, "But she's shaken. We've got her under observation 24-7."

Burns raises the question, "So they probably think she knows something about them."

Marin wonders aloud, "But why would Saunders identify her to you? That doesn't make sense."

Burns answers, "That's why I've got to talk with her."

McEwen agrees, "OK, I'll set it up. Give me an hour and then I'll call you back. She trusts me."

"Fine, anything else I need to know?"

Marin bobs his head a few times.

"Agent Marin has something else to add."

"I'm listening, what is it?"

"We know that they ... that would be Whitehead,

Saunders, and Rose … keep some rooms at a private club that are used to entertain certain business guests who they have relationships with."

Burns cuts in, "You're talking escorts as part of the business package, right?"

Marin agrees, "From what we can determine. No evidence to prove it yet."

McEwen breaks into the conversation, "They'd deny it for sure, claiming it's not what it looks like. That it's nothing sexual, just conversation and company for weary men and women who just need a break."

Burns lets out a hysterical laugh. "Sorry, but …." There is a slight pause, and then he continues, "Anything else?"

McEwen looks at Marin who shakes his head, no, "nothing from us. What about from your end?"

"Nothing at my end."

"I'll call you in an hour."

Later the same day, Detective Burns and Whitney Danica sit across from each other in a small family run restaurant that habitually has at least an hour long waiting line for lunch … combine quality food with reasonable prices and you've got the beginnings of a successful business. And, when you add above average portions with courteous service you've got a winner. It's now mid-afternoon and the lunch crowd has left.

Whitney looks around, and then smiles at him, "Interesting place. I wouldn't have figured it out by its appearance and location in town."

"Go figure." He finds it impossible not to return a

smile like hers. He's taken back by her good looks. Her appearance came up on him like a fog slowly creeping on shore, invisible at first, but once he was face-to-face with her, it was unmistakable. He swallows and then takes a sip of water.

"McEwen said it was important. What is it that you want to know?"

"Everything you know about them."

She gives him another one of her door-opening smiles. "That's quite broad, can you be more specific?"

"What I'm about to tell you is not for the public. Understood?"

She nods her head, "Got it."

"We're looking into the death of one of their employees … I guess I should say a former employee."

Whitney frowns. Her face goes stone-like, "Who?"

"Lynda Ackerman." He leans back in the booth.

"No." Her voice raises a pitch to reveal her surprise, but not loud enough for anyone other than the two of them to hear. "No," she repeats, but this time in disbelief.

"Yes, I'm sorry to be the one to tell you." His stare is more of an intent look than anything else. "Did you know her?"

"Very little, not much, almost not at all," she says as she nervously touches her ear with the thumb of her right hand.

"I wonder why Fred Saunders told me something quite different." This time his stare is more seriously looking.

"He did?" She hears her stomach growl.

"Oh, yes he definitely did."

"Specifically what did he say?" She leans forward.

"We were talking about his relationship with the deceased. He said you knew something about that."

"He admitted that to you?" Her eyes open wide.

"Listen, Miss Danica, I'm not going to play he said this, you said that. I'm here with you because he said you knew about his affair with her. Don't you find that interesting he would say that?"

"Very much so." She leans back into the booth. "Detective, just think about this. He's a married man with a five year old daughter who admitted to having an affair with an employee who now is dead." She twists her nose. "If I were investigating this case, he'd be the prime suspect. For goodness sake, he's the President of the WRS. Doesn't it seem reasonable that maybe she was intending to blackmail him, and the only way to prevent that from happening was to kill her! Huh?"

"Unfortunately, only in the movies is the trail of information so obvious. It might be difficult to understand, but in real life, it's much more complicated."

She lets out a breath of air. "And what is it that I can do for you?"

"Did you know he was having an affair with her?"

"Yes."

"How did you know?"

She lies, "It was understood by many employees of WRS, but nobody said anything about it."

"Does that include you?"

"Hell, no, I confronted him when I found out!"

"He's your boss, isn't he?"

"Yeah, he is, so what."

"I'd say that was a bold move on your part."

"I wouldn't."

"OK, what did you say?"

"Honestly, I don't remember the exact words, but something like, you're a piece of shit for betraying your wife." She feels her body tense with anger. "What kind of husband does that to his wife?"

"Are you married?"

"What?"

"I asked if you are married."

"What does that have to do with this? I'm not the one under suspicion." She pauses and looks him directly in his eyes, a glare that could melt iron. "Are you insane? I had nothing to do with this!"

"Please answer my question."

"I was married but not anymore."

"What happened?"

"Are you now my counselor?"

"Please, just answer the question."

"He walked out on me, the stupid son-of-a-bitch."

"So, he betrayed you." His voice is solemn, and even a bit saddened.

She swallows, significantly calmed down all of a sudden. Her head is slightly tilted towards the booth's tabletop. "Yes he did." Her face is sad looking.

"Is there anything else you think I might need to know?"

Slowly she lifts her head to face him, still cheerless and gloomy looking. She moves her lips without saying anything, and then the words come out. "He doesn't like me. I don't know why, but I can tell when someone doesn't like me. You know what I mean." She waits to see if he understands.

He nods his head in agreement without saying a word.

"His father-in-law is a good man, nothing like the son-in-law. I don't know how the creep got into the family. I haven't met his wife, but she puts up with his bullshit and tolerates it for some reason, or she's as rotten as him." She pauses, and then continues, "You did know his father-in-law is Charles Whitehead, the C. E. O. of WRS?"

"Yeah," his voice is soft and low.

"Are you gonna talk with her?"

He blinks once, "And who's that?"

"His wife, who the hell do you think I'm talking about?" She didn't have a high opinion of Burns when she first met him and nothing has changed except time.

While not knowing her at all when they first met, he feels even more uncomfortable with her now. He ignores her question. "Thanks for cooperating with me on this investigation. Should I need to talk with you again, I hope you'll agree." He forces a smile that fools no one.

She decides to keep her thoughts private for the time being. She swings her body out from the booth, stands and leaves him alone without saying another word.

Now sitting alone at the booth, he pulls out his cell to make a call. He hears her pick up.

"McEwen."

"This is Burns." He waits for a response that does not come so he says, "She's quite a character."

"It takes something to get used to her."

"And you trust her."

"Oh yeah … but there's still plenty of time for her to let you down."

"She's convinced Saunders did it, more emotional than evidence driven."

"What do you think?"

"I'm not sure." His vacant eyes look past the spot where Whitney had sat as if she hadn't even been there.

"What's next?"

"Lisa Saunders, his wife."

The next day Burns meets with Lisa Saunders at the same small family run restaurant at about the same time of his last meeting with Whitney at the same booth.

"Thanks for seeing me so quickly." He smiles. This time he is less nervous than he was with Whitney.

Lisa's lackluster eyes never stray from her face, and her voice is strong and clear, "Whatever I can do to help. It's just awful what happened to her ... such a lovely person. Fred told me."

"When was the last time you saw Lynda Ackerman?"

"She was at the volunteers' office doing odds and ends of things that nobody else seemed interested in wanting to do. She was such a wonderful person like that, no complaining, always positive and optimistic."

"And when was that?"

"I'm not sure, maybe this past weekend or maybe longer ago. It could have been late on a weekday as well. We don't have timecards and people don't officially check in and out. It's all volunteers."

"But others can vouch that she was there."

"Definitely ... of course ... why is that important?" Lisa looks at Burns with inquisitive eyes that seem to tell him she knows everything he's feeling and is reading his thoughts even before he speaks the words.

"I need to be able to confirm people's whereabouts around the time Lynda Ackerman was murdered. It's standard detective procedure, nothing more." His curious look seems to upset Lisa.

"What's this really about?"

"Like I said, it's normal investigative procedure. You seem upset."

Her lip quivers ever so slightly. "I'm – I'm just a little nervous. I've never been near anything like this before. I'm sorry if I was out of line." She glances away for a split second.

"And then she left."

Lisa clears her throat, "Yes."

"And when was that?"

"I don't know. Like I said before, volunteers come and go all the time. We don't keep track. But I imagine she had a prior appointment she had to keep." She shrugs her shoulders, "I'm just assuming. I really don't know."

Burns twists his body in the booth. "Now what I'm about to say might upset you."

Lisa mimics his body twist, and then touches her hair with the fingers of her left hand. She keeps quiet.

"How is your marriage?"

"Huh?"

"How are you and your husband getting along? Is it a solid marriage or are you having any problems?"

"What the hell is that any of your business?" Her voice is raised with anger. She is incensed with the implication. She leans over the table. "Are you married?"

"No."

"Then you have no idea how difficult it is to keep a marriage healthy for long periods of time. Both have to work their asses off to keep it going." She leans back, fixating her heated eyes on him all the while. She crosses her arms over her chest.

"I agree. I don't have any idea how difficult it is." He waits for her to jump in but she stays frozen in place. "So you're saying your marriage is at a rocky point in time?"

"I'm not saying anything to you about my marriage, absolutely nothing! It's none of your business!"

Burns decides to step up the conversation. "So you know that your husband, Fred, was having an affair with Lynda, the woman who has been murdered." He nips at his lower lip.

Lisa abruptly squirms out from behind the booth, stands to face Burns with her hands on her hips. "You're a low-life bastard! You get your kicks from others' hardships! You're pathetic!" She turns and walks away leaving him sitting alone by himself in the same booth in the same restaurant for the second consecutive time with a woman.

CHAPTER 8

Doctor Denise Joy's office is smaller than Whitney's regular therapist's office, who is off to a conference, and thus not available to see her at this time. There is a small desk that shows off its worn age. Nicks and scratches everywhere but that's what comes with getting older. Some refer to it as character. Imagine if desks could talk! There are scattered piles of paper everywhere … on the desk, on the floor, on shelves of a bookcase, and on a chair in the corner of the room. Whitney's first impression is not favorable of the fill-in for her regular therapist, but there's no sense of complaining. She has to talk with someone in private. Then she scans the wall right above Joy's head to spot the therapist's academic credentials … B. S., M. B. A., M. D. and J. D. … she reconsiders her earlier thought.

"You must be Ms. Whitney Danica," Joy says as she looks down at a scrap of paper on her desk. She stands but she remains behind the desk, extends her hand for a firm handshake. "I'm Doctor Joy. Please take a seat." She nods to the only empty chair that is across from the desk. "How can I help you?"

Whitney isn't at all completely sure she made the right

decision by making the appointment, but she figures since she's here, she'll go through with it.

Joy sits down first that signals to Whitney the clock has just started.

"Thank you for seeing me so quickly." She takes her seat as expected but still a wee bit skeptical of Joy's manner ... brisk and business like, not like what she's experienced before with her primary therapist, yet exactly how she conducts her meetings. Maybe there's a silver lining hidden someplace?

Joy grabs a nearby yellow legal pad in front of her. Her behavior is proficient and resolute.

Whitney keeps watching her, coming to the conclusion that she is the right person to talk with after all; no longer thinking it was a mistake as she earlier thought.

"Please tell me the situation." Her smile is mostly friendly but with a thin layer of frost as if to say, 'let's get on with it ... we're both busy people.'

"Uh ... I'm not sure where to begin."

"Let's start with your full name, age, and address."

"Whitney Danica, 31 years old, and I live at 1223 Prill Street, apartment 7."

"What do you do?"

"I specialize in marketing and promotion for WRS ... they're headquartered in the City."

"And how long have you been with WRS?"

"Seven years, if you count the time with my former Company that was recently bought out by WRS."

Joy efficiently writes on the yellow legal pad all the while each of them exchange information. "And why are you here today?"

Whitney's clears her throat, "I've been sexually harassed."

Joy shows no sign of disturbance or surprise, but completely impartial not to take sides. She pops her head up towards Whitney for a split second, "Tell me the circumstances." Then she drops her eyes towards the yellow legal pad of paper.

"My boss came on to me." Whitney swallows and blinks once.

"And what is the name of your boss?"

"Fred Saunders. He's the President of WRS, and he's my boss." She talks fast as if she doesn't want Joy to hear what she said, but that's not the case. Whitney is nervous.

"Uh-huh, when did this happen?" Joy continues to show no sign of amazement as she continues taking notes.

"A week or so ago."

"Why did you wait until today?"

"I wasn't sure I wanted to talk about it."

"And why was that?"

"I wanted to forget it … forever."

"Somethings are more difficult to forget than other things in our lives."

"Also, I thought no one would believe me."

"And why's that?"

"I can't prove anything."

"OK, we'll come back to that later on. But go on, tell me as much detail of what happened on that particular day."

"Since he's my boss, it's not unusual for him to call a meeting at any time of the day or any time of the week. That's just how it is at higher levels in most companies, at least that's how it is at WRS."

"So, he called this meeting."

"Yes."

"And you two were alone?"

"Yes."

"OK. Where did the meeting take place?"

"In his office after everyone left for the day."

"And what time would that have been?"

"Six, maybe just a little past six."

"No assistant around and no cleaning personnel there at the time?"

"Not that I was aware of."

"OK, go on."

"We talked a little while about my idea for a Company Blog."

"So the Company Blog was something new, something that you suggested?"

"Yes, it was going to be … it IS going to make the Company really successful. The C. E. O. really likes it." Her eyes light up with pleasure. Her voice is excited as well.

"Sounds as if this is something you're quite proud of?"

A big smile beams across her face. "Yes, very proud."

"Go on."

"But he wasn't as enthused as the C. E. O. or me."

"How do you know that?"

"He told me he was skeptical about its economic value, and that I had to show him, to give him some proof."

"Like metrics or benchmarking against competitors or something else?"

Whitney is surprised at Joy's understanding of business. "So, you know what I'm talking about?"

"Well, yeah. We all manage projects when we run a business regardless of what the business is, even in health care." Joy grins and then her face goes neutral. "So, what happened?"

"I figured he wanted me to show him the research I'd done. You know … the numbers. I had prepared a business plan with a few visuals to show him all of this."

"OK, go on."

"But he wanted something else."

"I'm listening."

"Well, like I said we talked a little about the Plan, and then he opened a bottle of wine. At first, I didn't even think about the wine. I just thought that was his way of conducting a business meeting after working hours. And then he came on to me."

"Can you be specific?"

"After he poured each of us a glass of wine, he walked toward a couch that was across the room in his office. He asked me to sit alongside him on the couch, which I did. Then we each took a sip of wine. But suddenly he reached over to put his hand on my knee and then started to kiss me. I was surprised, so I pulled back and said that this was not appropriate." She swallows. "How much detail do you want?"

"Just be general for now. He initiated this?"

"Definitely."

"And what was your reaction?"

"Like I said, I was surprised. I felt uncomfortable. Hell, this was supposed to be a business meeting! He's a married man!"

"What was the general atmosphere right before this happened?"

"A regular business meeting like the ones during the day, in a conference room, with others attending."

"And then it changed that quickly."

"Now you want some details?"

Joy nods affirmatively.

"OK, here's some. He made suggestive remarks about me ... how good I looked ... that I must exercise regularly ... how happy he was to have me as part of his team ... that there would be out-of-town business trips we'd probably have to take together, just the two of us ... that he wanted to make sure we were compatible with each other. Is that enough?"

"Describe your boss ... looks, age, and so forth?"

"I'd say the same age as me, good looking man, a good dresser, polite when I've met him in groups of others."

"No sexual overtones, no sexual jokes, flirtations, innuendoes, and the like?"

"Not towards me."

"What about towards others ... men or women?"

Whitney wonders if she should mention Saunders' alleged relationship with Lynda Ackerman and her recent death.

Joy probes, "You're holding something back that may be important. I'm not saying it is, but I won't know unless you tell me. What are you thinking about?"

"It is suspected that he and one of MY Department employees were having an affair."

"Only an allegation, nothing proven, nothing charged, only purported, is that right?"

"Yes."

"Anything else about this assumed situation?"

"The woman was found dead in a dumpster a few days ago. The police think she was murdered."

"I see." She continues to take notes. "Let's get back to your evening business meeting with your boss. Give me some details."

"After he touched my knee and started to kiss me, I pulled back. He was persistent because he reached again for my leg to try to get his hand up my dress. I kicked away. Then he stood and unzipped his pants to expose himself. I was shocked and confused. I didn't know what to do. Hell, there was no one in the office except the two of us and I felt trapped." She takes in a deep breath of air.

Joy looks up at Whitney during her pause, thinking she'd naturally continue, but she doesn't. "Did he literally expose his penis? Did you see it?"

"Yes, yes, I did. Then he reached over to grab my hand and said something like 'you'll like how it feels' but I really don't remember. Like I said before, I was shocked. Nothing like this has ever happened to me before. I didn't know what to do."

"So you didn't say anything to him?"

"Like what? I don't remember."

"I'm just asking if you remember saying anything to him at this point."

"I might have said something, but I don't remember! How many times do I have to tell you? I don't remember!"

"What happened next?"

"I stood up."

"And …?"

"He pushed me back onto the couch. His penis was just hanging out of his pants."

"So you didn't want to have sexual intercourse with him?"

"I was afraid!"

"Afraid of what?"

"I didn't want to get involved with my married boss. He was trying to rape me! Don't you get it?"

Joy looks at Whitney, her eyes sympathetic yet cool and objective at the same time. "So, you didn't have sexual intercourse or oral intercourse with him because he was your boss and he was married."

"Yes, I've already said that!"

"Nothing else?"

"Like what?"

"Like, everyone is going to eventually know that you had sexual intercourse with your boss in his office, and there wouldn't be any way to keep it quiet. It would eventually get out."

Whitney thinks about it for a short time. "What you're really asking me if I thought I could get away with it ... to have sex with my boss in his office. Is that it?"

"It is what you think it is. Is that it?"

Whitney's voice is subdued, "Maybe."

"Did you do anything that was not for self-protection?"

"No! I did not come on to him!"

"And you're sure about that."

"Absolutely."

"OK, what happened next?"

"He picked up his wine glass that was on a small table in front of the couch and threw it at me. By then I was standing and thinking how to get out of his office. His aim was off and so I ran to the door to leave."

"Anything else?"

"I was really upset."

"Have you told this to anyone other than me?"

"No."

"Why?"

"It just didn't occur to me."

Joy shows slight surprise with a frown, "No one?"

Whitney pauses, "Honestly, I don't have anyone close to talk with about stuff like this." She pauses again, "I just want this to go away."

"And you didn't report this to your H. R. representative?"

"Hell no!"

"Why's that?"

"He's worthless."

"You should have gone on record just the same."

"OK, OK, but I didn't."

"What's going to happen when you return to work and have to meet with your boss again?"

"I'm not going to quit, if that's what you're implying."

"I'm not implying anything. I'm just asking a question about what do you think will happen when you return to work and have to meet with your boss again."

"I'll get through it."

Joy looks at her watch. "We're running out of time. Is there anything else?"

"I know it's not what you do, but I do see your J. D. Degree on the wall. Do you practice law as well?"

"I'm bar certified. Sometimes the medical and legal cases overlap. What are you really asking me?"

"Do I have a legal case against him for sexual harassment?"

"That could be argued, and if successful it would be a

jury case. And with a jury you really don't know what will happen at a trial. But from what you've told me, I don't think your case is strong."

"What?"

"I'm just telling you that in my opinion your case is not strong. I didn't make the Law."

"Then the Law should be changed!"

"Listen to reason."

Whitney turns her head away from Joy for a quick second and then back to face her. She isn't happy. "Go on."

"The 1964 Civil Rights Act makes it unlawful for an employer to discriminate against employees based on an individual's gender. Title VII of the Act indicates that unwelcome sexual advances, request for sexual favors, and other verbal or physical conduct of a sexual nature constitutes sexual harassment when any one of three specific conditions is met. The more difficult sexual harassment issues have been in the area of hostile work environment because there still remains confusion about what specific activities constitute the offense. To sustain a finding of hostile work environment of sexual harassment, it is generally required that the harassment be unwelcomed by the harassed, the harassment be gender based, the harassment be sufficiently severe or pervasive to create an abusive work environment, the harassment affect a term, condition, or privilege of employment, and the employer had actual or constructive knowledge of the sexually hostile work environment and took no prompt or adequate remedial action." She pauses, wondering if she's given Whitney too much information too quickly, "any questions?"

"It's a hell of a lot of information to take in, but I think I've got the gist. Go on."

"From what you've told me, I don't think you'll be able to prove a hostile work environment based on this single incident. It's a matter of she said, he said. There were no witnesses."

"So, I'm screwed." Whitney's eyes pop open realizing what she's literally said. "You know what I mean."

"I'm just giving you my advice. But if you want to file an official E. E. O. C. sexual harassment claim against your Company or your boss, then you'll need to contact the local E. E. O. C. office who'll walk you through the process."

"Do you believe me?"

"Whether I believe you or not is not the issue. It's whether you can prove it."

"And how do I do that?"

"Be honest, have sympathetic listeners, and retain one hell of a lawyer."

She sounds defeated, "Right."

"Maybe this will help. Let me review. First, you claim you got into an intimate situation with your male boss, but turned him down, something that is not an easy sell to anybody, especially since you didn't report it to your H. R. rep. Second, if you bring a lawsuit against your Company, you could get fired for a variety of legitimate reasons, could easily be transferred or ignored until you leave on your own. Third, if you bring a direct lawsuit against them, you'll be looking at most likely three years before the case goes to trial, if in fact it advances to a trial. The likelihood is it won't get that far. The courts are backed up with sexual harassment claims made by both women and men. If you're working then you've got income for expenses, but if you're out of work the likelihood that another company will hire you is remote."

"Shit."

"That's just how it is." Joy pauses, "Do you want me to go on?"

"Sure, how much worse can it be?"

Joy ignores the comment. "Also, during those three years, you'll go through emotional turmoil. It's very difficult to live a normal life. Fourth, I'm not sure what damages you could claim have occurred to you. You're still employed by them without any financial damage. No one knows this happened so there isn't any professional embarrassment that I detect presently. You might plead emotional distress but that will cost you to bring in a medical expert to attest to that, something that is very difficult to prove. It's going to cost you thousands of dollars to retain an attorney, and if you win, they along with taxes to the Feds and State, you'll be left with little money. Yes, it's all taxable income. But, you're 31 years old, relatively young at this point. Add three years and you'll be 34, also relatively young. It's obvious your decision, not mine to make."

"Damn, and this time I mean it. I'm screwed." Whitney's face is full of sadness and anger. "Would you take my case if I asked?"

"Definitely not."

Whitney slumps back into her chair. "Life is not fair."

"But these are the truths of a lawsuit."

"It's just not just." Her voice is soft as she admits defeat.

"The law is about finding a pathway to settle the quarrel. Don't make it more than it really is."

Whitney looks up towards the white popcorn ceiling, blinks a few times and then lets out a puff of air. "I want to go through with this."

Joy looks at her watch again, stands, and says, "Listen, we are now out of time." She pauses for a quick second and continues. "If you go through with this, your life will be public. You'll have to tell your attorney everything about your personal life as difficult as that might be. Lawyers don't want to be surprised hearing something that you've kept hidden from them. Do you understand?" Her look is intense.

Whitney nods a yes.

"Here's some practical advice. Go through your office and remove anything personal. Change your passwords on everything. Do the same for your home computer if you have one."

"Do you really think this is necessary?" She frowns.

"I KNOW it's necessary."

"But you said you wouldn't take my case."

"That still stands. I'm only suggesting a few protective measures that almost any trial lawyer worth anything would advise. Take it or leave it."

Once outside the Office building Whitney walks alone on the sidewalk thinking about the conversation with Joy. While she wasn't sure what to expect from the therapist she isn't happy now as it turned out. Hell, she has the risk of losing her job, not working for another company in her specialty or maybe ever again in a professional capacity. In essence, she thinks, her life as she's known it could be over.

Questions and her point of view on the situation never occurred to her. Why hadn't she told someone about Saunders' sexual harassment, at least Karen, her most trusted Company employee? She could have talked with Jesse, the male escort from a short time ago, but really, is that what these guys do for a living … providing insight into messed up women's lives?

She could have talked with Hank Rose, WRS's Chief Legal Counsel. He'd know for sure what to do, or would he just push it away as something incidental? And then there's Charles Whitehead, the C. E. O., who seems to value her Company Blog proposal. He'd listen objectively, or would he? Probably not since it's one of his direct reports as President, and from a personal point-of-view his son-in-law.

She thinks about how she might have prevented it from happening, but then she suddenly realizes that during one of their first encounters she said to Saunders something that implied she probably couldn't get to first base with him if she tried. Then another time comes to mind when she squeezed his hand just a little and then released her grip. Would he remember those times if he was cross-examined?

She continues to walk slowly considering possibilities. Then she shakes her head concluding it likely that anything she might do now wouldn't make a difference because in the end as Joy clearly stated, it is her word against his. And he's the one with the formal power, the authority that the Company would listen to. He's the one with allies, not her. Maybe she should be the one to talk with Samuelson? No way! So, does this mean that she simply forget about it like Joy suggested, or is there something else she can do?

Maybe Saunders has already filed an internal complaint

against her alleging she came on to him with Samuelson, the dim-witted H. R. Director? Maybe there's an internal investigation going on right now? Maybe there's nothing going on because Saunders' couldn't possibly want to be part of an internal employee relations sexual harassment claim, so he hasn't said anything. He doesn't want to lose his power base and perhaps as importantly if not more important, he doesn't want to disenfranchise his father-in-law. Suddenly she stops walking.

"That's it," she says aloud to herself. "He's not going to do diddly-squat because he wants to do everything possible to keep it hush-hush. He probably even thinks that I'm going to keep my trap shut as well!"

She feels good for the time being as she resumes walking, yet still thinking to herself. Then, unexpectedly she realizes she's back in front of the Company's office building.

Now headed back to her office she stops at the door, surprised to see Saunders there, talking to someone on her phone.

His eyes pop out to notice her, and then he says to the other party on the phone, "I'll call you back."

Whitney asks, "What's up?"

"Oh, I was just looking for you, and once in your office it dawned on me I promised to make a call back."

She knows he's lying and so does he know that she knows, "really?" She wonders who he was talking with.

"Yeah, really."

"Why were you looking for me?"

"About the Company Blog, we've got preliminary funding to start it. I'm very happy for you."

She's impressed with his control over his emotions at this very time, but she's got something to tell him. "That's great news. And I've got something to tell you." She grins.

"And what's that?"

"I've decided to retain a law firm to represent me." She hopes she's convincing.

"Oh, for what?"

Her voice is controlled, "Due to job sexual harassment from the President of the Company, Fred Saunders."

"Me, you're out of your mind!"

"Perhaps."

"And when did this alleged incident happen?"

"You've forgotten?" She stares, "In your office, the wine, the indecent behavior, the intimidation, your sexual exposure and attack on me."

He throws up his hands, "You'll never prove it ... your word against mine ... never prove it ... never happened."

"I'm betting I will. Title VII of the 1964 Civil Rights Act prohibits sexual harassment in the workplace. Did you know that?"

"Whitney ..."

"I've thought about this for a while."

"You're making a big mistake."

"Why's that?"

"It never happened. You can't possibly win."

"We'll see."

"There isn't a hell of a chance."

"It's the right thing to do."

"And you're lying."

"This is my decision."

"You'd be putting yourself in a difficult position."

"The way I see it, it's you and Company who are in a difficult position."

"What do you want?"

"You mean to go away?"

"I didn't say that."

"Justice is what I want."

He puffs out a little air, "Don't we all." He quickly leaves her office headed towards Whitehead's.

"Boss, we've got a problem." Saunders steps into Whitehead's office, and closes the door behind. Rose is seated a few feet away in a comfortable chair. He spots the Chief Legal Counsel. "I'm glad you're here too."

"This better be important." Whitehead's forehead frowns.

"Whitney is claiming I sexually harassed her. It's a total bogus claim. She wants something in return to make it go away." He takes a seat in a vacant chair.

Rose asks, "Did you?"

"Hell no! I'm innocent, but she's a loose-cannon." His lie is convincing for the moment, but will it survive?

Whitehead asks, "What does she want?"

"She wants to file a sexual harassment claim."

"That's not what I mean!"

"But it's what she told me."

"Does she realize that would be unwise?" Rose asks. "She probably has no idea what the process is for this kind of claim."

Saunders replies, "I think she does. I suspect she's already talked with a law firm to represent her."

Rose raises a question, "Who's the firm?"

"She didn't say."

Rose continues, "Then maybe she's bluffing."

"I don't think so. She's serious."

Whitehead asks, "And you're one hundred percent positive there is nothing you've done to her?"

He continues to be persistent of his innocence, "Absolutely positive."

Whitehead turns to Rose, "What's the process?"

"She'll probably talk with Samuelson, the H. R. guy to file an internal complaint. Then she'll file a formal charge with the E. E. O. C. to go on record. Actually since there isn't a Federal E. E. O. C. office in our State, the filing will be with a 706-Agency, specifically the Department of Fair Employment and Housing. They'll notify us that a claim has been filed. Then we would do our due diligence in investigating the internal complaint thoroughly and quickly to establish our position of not tolerating anything like this in the workforce. I don't think Samuelson has ever done this before. He's essentially an admin type we put in the job. Also, I don't think he's got the brains. But that's something else. I'll handle it all myself."

Whitehead turns to Saunders, "Again, you're totally positive the internal investigation will show nothing."

"Definitely."

Whitehead keeps his stare towards Saunders. "You said nothing happened … right?"

"Yes."

Whitehead turns to Rose, "And how soon with the E. E. O. C. get involved?"

"Thirty days from her filing. They'll assign someone specific to the case. And from that point forward that's who we'll be in contact with. They'll take about ninety days to finish their investigation, and then make a ruling. They'll definitely want to talk with us and other employees as necessary."

Saunders interrupts, "It's a witch hunt!"

Rose shakes his head, no, "It's the process that is used. This means that our internal investigation must be thorough, impartial, and reliable. We can't bribe anyone to say something. We can't promise openly or subtlety anything to anyone. That would be the kiss of death."

Whitehead continues, "Give me the specifics."

"Once she files with them, the 706-Agency, The Department of Fair Employment and Housing contacts us within 10 business days after she files to ask us a few questions. Is the claimant part of a protected class under relevant statue? Was the claimant treated adversely? Was the claimant's performance satisfactory? Were others not in the protected class treated differently, more favorably? We deny any wrong doing."

Whitehead continues his questioning, "What happens next?"

"They screen the claim for any wrong doing. If they believe there is nothing to the case, they dismiss it and give the claimant a right-to-sue-letter which means she can hire an attorney to go to court. This can be expensive for her."

Whitehead asks, "Is that it?"

Rose replies. "Oh no, if they think there is merit to

the claim under the 1964 Civil Rights Act, Title VII, they investigate the allegation thoroughly. If their investigation finds reasonable cause, then they'll recommend mediation where both parties have to agree on the mediator. If both parties agree on mediation then they follow mediation rules. If the 706-Agency finds cause, then they try to conciliate. If that is unsuccessful, then they can impose damages to the defendant. Up to this point there is no cost to the claimant. In this instance it means Whitney doesn't pay for anything, but we'll be paying for all our costs."

Whitehead puffs out a breath of air, "Crap!"

"Yeah, it is what it is. Do I continue?"

"Sure, we all need to know what we're getting into." Whitehead throws an unfriendly smirk at Fred.

Rose continues. "At any time each party can appeal the cause finding up to the E. E. O. C. Commission itself. If Title VII remedies are exhausted, the relevant District Court reviews the case as de novo, which means as if it had not been previously addressed. In order to appeal a Court judgement, the appealing party must prove that the Court made an error during the trial, such as not allowing relevant information, and that this error, if not made, would have changed the outcome of the trial. If the Appeals Court finds in favor of the appealing party, the case is sent back to the original Court. If the Appeals Court finds in favor of the respondent, the judgement stands, and it is now up to the appealing party to further appeal to the next level, all the way to the Supreme Court. We're in the 9th Circuit Court, sometimes referred to as the 9th Circus Court because of its liberal tendencies. This entire process can take at least three years to complete."

Whitehead looks frustrated. He turns to Saunders. "And once again I ask, you're sure you've never made any sexual overtones, jokes, physical contact, and so forth towards her and any other employee that could be construed as sexual harassment?" His frown is piercing.

"She's a bitch, a money hungry bitch!"

"That wasn't my question. Do I need to repeat it?"

"No, I've done nothing wrong!" Saunders kicks the side of a small table in front of him.

Whitehead yells, "If any of this goes public we are screwed! How much time is there?" He looks at Rose.

"Probably within three to four days, depending on how fast the 706-Agency does it's paperwork from the date she files her claim.

Whitehead turns to Rose, "Somebody's got to kick some sense into her. Does she really know what she's doing?"

Rose shakes his head, yes, "It seems as if she knows exactly what she's doing."

Whitehead is angry. "We have substantial publicity as well as potential financial loss if this turns out to be true."

Saunders interrupts, "But it's all false." His insistence of innocence remains strong.

Whitehead ignores the comment as he turns to Rose. "Who do we know in the legal system to step in?"

"That's a very bold move. I advise against it."

"And what specifically do you advise we do?"

"Follow the rule of law, simple and straightforward."

Saunders interrupts, "And put me in the mouth of a lion?"

"The Courts are very good at what they do. Let them

exonerate you in the eyes of the justice system. Don't mess with the law."

Whitehead laughs, "As if we haven't done that before."

"This is much too serious, in my legal opinion," answers Rose.

Saunders adds, "She doesn't have a case! She's lying!"

Whitehead asks to both men, "So trying to make a deal with her is out of the question? Is that what you're both saying?"

Rose is the first to respond. "No, I'm not saying that. Everybody always wants something. I'm willing to bend the rule of law. We've been successful before, but this is different. I advise against it. If Fred is truthful, and I have no reason to believe he isn't, then we've got nothing to hide. In fact, when we're exonerated, it might even bump our financial standing even higher."

Whitehead turns to Saunders, "And what do you say?" His stare is firm and glaring.

Saunders swallows. He has no alternative, "I didn't do anything."

Whitehead says, "Ok then. Let's prepare our case against her."

Saunders looks around at the two men. "Is that it?"

Rose nods towards Whitehead who says, "That should do it for now."

Saunders stands, but hesitates before leaving the office. "Are you sure there's nothing else?"

Whitehead is curt, "Yes."

Now alone with one another Whitehead says to Rose, "We've got to keep her."

"Yes, of course."

"She's got experience and is a fireball!"

"What do you want me to do?"

"I want you to find out what really happened, if anything at all. I want the truth, only the truth. Then, I want it resolved."

"OK."

"Do whatever is necessary." Whitehead pauses, and then says, "You know what I mean."

"OK."

"I appreciate you talking with me here, away from the office." Rose's smile is genuine.

Whitney's smile is guarded, careful not to let her guard down. "We all need to eat lunch, and I've haven't been here before." She looks around. "This is a nice place."

"Yes, it is … a private club. I'm happy it works for you."

She grabs the cloth napkin lying in front of her to dab a bit of moisture forming on her upper lip.

"I recommend the special. That's of course, if you enjoy baked salmon with artichokes, carrots and mashed potatoes. It's one of my favorites." His voice is calm and reassuring to her ears, just as he intends it to be.

"That's fine with me. I'll take your advice." Her smile has loosened up a bit.

Rose signals to a waiter standing a few feet away to come closer as he asks her a question, "something to drink?"

She hesitates for a quick second putting aside the desire for a shot of whiskey. "Unsweetened ice tea is fine."

"Excellent." He turns to the waiter, "Two specials with unsweetened ice tea for each of us."

Once the waiter leaves the table Rose takes a sip of water before he talks. "I'd like to give you some advice, if I may." His eyes are warm.

She thinks twice having a hard time settling on his courteous and refined behavior, something she hadn't considered until now. "Sure."

"And some feedback from Charles and me."

She nods a yes. Her heart ticks up a wee bit.

"You're young looking and beautiful. You're shrewd in many ways but dumb in others. While you may not like him or even respect him, Saunders is still your boss. What I'm about to say about men doesn't only apply to men. Women do it as well, but I'm only referring to men right now. They tend to take advantage of situations for personal gain. They sometimes ignore the law, in other words they intentionally break it thinking they can get away with it. And yes, it's immoral but yes, it happens. It's unavoidable. It's life. You're promiscuous, I know, you've been checked out, investigated. We even have your D. N. A. from a variety of sources." He doesn't wait for a response in spite of seeing a look of shock on her face, so he continues. "Said another way, we, that is Charles and me, know who you are. You're a bit of a control freak, something that Charles and I can relate to." He grins and then chuckles. "We see that in ourselves as well. And when things don't go your way, you get pissed which makes you wanting to get even. Now, that's not good. Trust me on that. You hate office politics unless you can create the rules. You think an E. E. O. C. sexual harassment lawsuit is going to settle it all, but you're very mistaken. It's going to backfire on you which will leave you worse off for it. Saunders may be a total asshole, disloyal to his wife, and a real prick. But he is the son-in-law of the C. E. O., which means something ... very much so. As long as Charles is C. E. O. he's going to stay loyal to him, but not for the reason you might think. It's because he doesn't want his daughter, whom he loves so much, to be hurt. I won't get into her situation, but she too is not who she claims to be. Maybe at some other time, if or when conditions change we can talk about that, but not now. It's a terrible thing what happened to Miss Ackerman but she probably threatened someone, maybe it was Saunders, maybe it was someone else, I don't know. Something she should had known better not to do. My advice to you is to apologize to Saunders, drop the E. E. O. C. charge, and get back to work." He takes a sip of water, his eyes still glued onto hers.

Whitney nods her head slightly to the left. "I can't do that."

"Too much self-respect?"

"Maybe, maybe not."

"Then what it is? Are you too much infatuated with being right?"

She doesn't sound convinced even to herself, "Could be."

"I've got much more advice, but honestly I don't think you'll take it."

"Like what?"

"Do what you do best and don't try to be something you're not."

"Like what?"

"Marketing, promotion, and the Company Blog is what you're good at. Avoid the politics. It's not who you are."

A modulated voice suddenly interrupts their conversation. "Excuse me, here are your luncheons. Is there anything else you need now?"

Rose looks at Whitney who shakes her head sideways, no. "That should do it for now."

As the waiter slightly bows his head he says, "Enjoy," and then slips away.

Whitney remains dazed from the feedback, in a way much too much to process here and now, but she tries her best to take it all in. She opens her mouth to say something but conveniently for her Rose cuts her off. He has more to say.

"Charles and I want you to stay with WRS. We've put together a new strategy that will help everyone out, and in this situation whatever Charles wants outdoes what anyone else wants. Consider Saunders not having a say in this matter." He waits to see how she responds.

She's sure she's heard it correctly, but she's also a skeptical person who is suspicious of seemingly good news. She's been betrayed one too many times. She manages to show off a pleasant smile that seems to signal to Rose to continue.

"You'll be an executive at the same level as Saunders, reporting directly to Charles. That's how he wants it." He catches a flicker from Whitney's left eye, revealing her surprise and satisfaction, so he continues. "Within 2 years we plan to take the Company public. You'll get 5 thousand shares with options for another 5 thousand more, and then 5 thousand per year options after that at 25 cents a share. The stock will be offered to the public at somewhere between

10 and 20 dollars a share. You'll be rich in a very short time. But you have to trust Charles and me. That's very important." He stops talking, looking for other signs from her that reveal herself.

Whitney doesn't realize that she fidgets nervously, mostly out of surprise. She's always wanted to be at the top of the heap but now that she hears it is a possibility if not probable, she begins to doubt it. She asks herself if she can really trust Charles and Rose. She forces to reassure herself that she can play with the big boys. Now calmed down, she says, "Put it in writing."

"Consider it done." He reaches over the table to shake her hand. "Welcome to the top of the mountain. You'll enjoy the view."

She firmly grabs his hand. She's sure she hasn't heard it before said exactly like that, but now that she has she believes she's known it all her life. "I won't let you and Charles down."

Later on that night, after sex, they remain uncharacteristically quiet. They seemed to have done what they had planned ... passionate but without feelings. That's how it is supposed to be between an escort and his client. This time, however, it seems different to Whitney. She smiles at Jesse, lying on his back, hands across his chest, waiting for her next instruction, as she typically does. He's totally content with that arrangement ... not much to worry about what to do and when ... just do it. But something unexpectedly happens.

Whitney turns onto her right side, facing her quiet lover,

and then she leans closer to him. Passionately, yet tenderly at the same time, she moves her lips all over his mouth, then his cheeks, nose, eyelids, forehead, ears, chin, and throat.

He starts to reciprocate with his hands moving to between her legs, when all of a sudden he unexpectedly feels her push his hands away.

"No," she whispers as she presses her left index finger over his lips.

He obediently obeys, wondering what she is up to. He is polite … that's part of the rules agreement.

Whitney continues moving her head downward towards his toes, all the while kissing and caressing him like he's never experienced before. Finally, when she's finished, she looks at Jesse squarely in the eyes, and whispers "I'm a changed woman."

Jesse's figures he's supposed to say something, not to let her comment go ignored … not the typical agreement between them, but what the hell, he's got nothing to lose. She's the client. "I'm listening."

She touches his face gently, feels the slight facial hair growth on his chin since his last shave, and starts talking. "I want to be a better person, but I don't know how."

Jesse thinks he's got the perfect response. "You sure are beautiful. Your intense brown eyes, the angle of your nose, cheekbones, and lips … those luscious lips. You've got the total package." He smiles thinking he's nailed the answer.

"That's not what I'm referring to."

He recovers quickly. "I know, but I don't know how to respond to what you've said. Tell me more."

"I want to go out on a real date with you. You know, dinner, a movie … to be seen together. I'd like that."

Jesse shrugs his shoulders. He still doesn't get what she means. "Sure, but that can be expensive."

"That's not the kind of date I mean."

"Oh."

"It'd be off the record … just you and me as a couple doing what couples do." She starts feeling a little sympathy for herself, more like pity, as if she is begging to be treated like a normal person.

"I don't know. You know the rules. I could get into trouble and lose my job."

"You'll find another job. You'll think of something."

"I don't know."

Whitney isn't happy with his level of cooperation and enthusiasm about the idea. She needs to try another approach. Suddenly she asks, "Have you ever been in love?"

"That's a personal question, another no-no."

"That's OK, I understand." She realizes she's crossed a few lines. It's fine with her if he doesn't want to talk about it. "To be honest, I once was in love, but vowed never to be again." She sees his face change from distant to sorrow. "But I want to be in love now and forever. And further, I'll promise never to betray him, never."

He figures he's got to keep the conversation impersonal, away from him. "Are you in touch with him?"

"No, but well he recently left a voice message saying he wanted to get back together with me."

"What's stopping you?"

"He's a prick!"

Jesse takes her hand in his. "Some people deserve a second chance … maybe everybody does."

"Not him! I'll never forgive him for what he did to me!"

Still holding her hand, he squeezes it gently as he says, "So much for being a better person."

"It isn't easy." In spite of some discomfort, she likes the conversation. She feels her breathing nicely settled into a good place.

There is a pause. Both are a little afraid of saying anything stupid to each other. The silence stretches out. Eventually Jesse says, "How do you feel about having a family?"

Whitney is surprised how comfortable she is with the question. Has she been waiting for someone to ask her? Is it a real cue, or is it bait that she'll be laughed at for taking seriously. She smiles, "I think I'd love it." She leans over to gently kiss him on the lips.

Jesse pulls Whitney down towards him, pressing their bodies close to each other.

"You're crazy," he whispers in her ear.

She thinks for a second. "I'll take that as a compliment." She wonders if she is only imaging how wonderful she feels, or if this is how it feels when you're in love. "If you weren't doing this, what would you be doing?"

He doesn't wait long to answer. "I like to help people."

"Oh, like a social worker, a doctor?"

"Could be, but it could be anything that helps people … physically, mentally, financially … you know."

"Then why don't you do it?"

He grins, "In a way, I am doing it now."

She gets his version of being an escort, "Very funny." She pauses, "So, you're happy."

"Oh, no, quite frustrated."

"Again, why don't you do it?"

"Fear of failure." He swallows hard, suddenly overcome with grief and realization that he shared such an important part of his life with her, something he's kept hidden for a long time. He struggles to hold back tears. He can barely say another word. "Lack of confidence ... you know ... the usual stuff."

Her head, resting on his chest just over his heart, feels the beat pick up. "I didn't mean to upset you."

Words come out slowly, "Not your fault."

"Let's talk about something else."

Relieved but not fully prepared to offer something specific he says, "Like what?"

She asks, "Do you like math?"

He frowns, thinks for a second or two, "No."

"I do. Equations, formulas, logic, everything fits together nicely. It's predictable."

"No surprises."

"Exactly ... Do you know about the Fibonacci sequence?"

"Be serious," he frowns.

She is enthused to explain. "The Fibonacci sequence is named after an Italian mathematician named Leonardo of Pisa, but the progression of numbers is known as Fibonacci for some reason. The Fibonacci sequence is a set of numbers that starts with a zero or a one, followed by a one, and goes on based on the rule that each number, called a Fibonacci number, is equal to the sum of the previous two numbers. Here's the example. Take the series of numbers 0, 1, 1, 2, 3, 5, 8, 13, 21, 34, for example. The next number is found by adding up the two numbers before it. For example 0 plus 1 equals 1, 1 plus 1 equals 2, 1 plus 2 equals 3, and so on." She continues to smile with gusto. "Isn't that the coolest thing?"

"It seems to you." His voice is apathetic.

"Do you want to know more?"

"Ah no, not now," He continues to show his lack of interest.

"I do like routine and patterns."

The topic is obviously a safe one for both of them to talk about, but of much more interest to her than to him.

Jesse looks up at the ceiling. "I'm taking classes online towards an M.B.A.."

"How's that going for you?"

"No face-to-face stuff. Faculty and students communicate online. I've just got to post my assignments each week by a specific day and time, and then wait for the feedback and grade. Usually I have to respond to questions that the faculty posts. Not much pressure. I can do the work when it best fits into my schedule. Nothing personal needed to share with other students and faculty ... strictly academic."

"So, no real brick-and-mortar classroom with students and faculty ... there's no eye-to-eye contact."

"Yeah, and it's so convenient."

"Is it from an accredited school?"

"Sure, at least that's my understanding. Why?"

"Some of these so-called academically accredited schools are fly-by-night. I wouldn't want you to get hurt. That's all." She touches his face again where she left off, feeling somehow reassured of something, but not sure what exactly that is.

Jesse asks, "Why did you do that?"

"Did I offend you?"

"Oh, no, just the opposite. But why did you do it?"

Whitney's voice is soft and sincere. "I don't know, it just happened, but it made me feel content."

"Me too," Jesse smiles. Then he shifts his body to face her, holds her face in both hands, and kisses her lips.

"What are you majoring in?"

"O. B.," he spiritedly answers.

"Huh?"

"Organizational Behavior. It's the study of an organization's values, purpose, mission, strategy, and all sorts of other things that are important to the organization. Sort of like the culture ... what makes it unique and therefore different from other organizations. When an employee understands an organization's culture, he or she can consciously decide to adapt to fit in. If the employee doesn't fit into how things are done within the organization, then there is a strong likelihood the employee will fail. In fact, studies have shown that most employee turnover is based on not fitting in to how things are done within the organization." He pauses, thinking she'd have a question by now, but when she doesn't he continues. "So, organizations, those who are authentic, share with the current employees and candidates for jobs who they are and what they're about. They're transparent, and create incentives and so forth to support who they are."

All Whitney says is, "Hmm, interesting." She's thinking about something but not yet willing to share it ... that she's been offered the opportunity of a lifetime to fit into the culture of WRS as an executive.

Jesse waits for some sort of response from her, but when nothing happens, he keeps quiet as well.

Whitney's thoughts drift elsewhere. She wants Jesse to feel her affection without any ifs, ands, or buts … no doubts. Only that she'll be there for him to do whatever he wants to do … how foolish or sensible it might be. But she'll never tell him any of this because she doesn't want to be rejected … to be left alone again … to feel hurt … to be betrayed. They say the first hurt is the worse, but she isn't interested in challenging that right now. She wouldn't know what to do … really what to do … if he told her he loved her, so she decides not to push the proverbial envelope. It's much safer that way.

But if he isn't willing to share his feelings with her, at least not now, why doesn't she say it to him? She thinks of a few reasons why. Could it be because her biological parents and then her adopted ones never said it to her … not even once, not even as an act of courtesy … that they loved her? Could it be that her former husband lied to her about his alleged endless love for her? Could it be that she now feels like crap that she told her former husband how much she loved him and now realizes that he betrayed her?

She decides not to surrender to love. They'll be no white flag raised right now.

Their eyes close and after a moment they both groan softy and together in rhythm. Then their eyes open at the same time finding each other looking intently at the other. They kiss again, gently, warm air moving between their mouths, pulling each closer to the other, not resisting. They burn with desire, yet they keep silent their own thoughts.

CHAPTER 9

A week has passed and Whitney has decided not to pursue a sexual harassment charge. The offer from WRS was too compelling to pass up.

She sits by herself in the outdoor patio area of *The Roasting Company* sipping a double expresso, mumbling something to herself that even she doesn't understand. Yet, inside her body she feels turmoil, confusion, and so much more than the peace and order she'd like to feel. Shouldn't she feel relieved? She turns her attention to a 20ish year old looking couple sitting close by whose discussion about something starts out in check but quickly heads south.

The female holds onto a local free weekly newsletter as she reads aloud an article to her male partner. "Get a load of this title." She adjusts her body in the metal chair before continuing. "Feminism takes center stage once again!" Her mouth remains wide open.

The male replies, "Don't tell me the writer, but I'm pretty sure I know who SHE is … Carol McFadden."

"It's that obvious?"

"Please. She's THE ultimate women hater."

The female begins to read the full article aloud. "A large company, that we'll refer to as Company-A, recently acquired a local company that will also remain anonymous. Shortly after the acquisition they promoted a highly competent woman from within the acquired company into an executive position based on her knowledge, skills, abilities, willingness, desires, and motivation. Bravo! But she didn't seem to like it … it wasn't enough … so she fabricated a sexual harassment incident against her male boss, the same person who was mentoring her. It seems her appetite to take down her male boss, and probably all men in the end, and assume their role is totally out of control. She's a whacko and very dangerous. Company-A will probably cave in to whatever her outlandish demands are in order to avoid litigation. And this babe will walk away with a truckload of money as she looks for her next victim. Stay tuned for more."

The male poses a question, "What's your take?"

She puts the paper flat down on the metal table. "It appears to be some sour grapes between her and the boss. What's new?" She shrugs her shoulders.

"Maybe the boss was simply trying to get to know his new direct report. You know, have a drink at lunch or something innocent like that."

She asks, "Although in this article it seems to be a boss-subordinate situation, what do you think about 'you can't go out with co-workers?'"

"Co-workers are peers, as you've already pointed out. The article is about a boss-subordinate relationship. That's very different. In the first instance there isn't any formal power difference between the two employees, but with the second instance there definitely is. I wouldn't call the boss-subordinate relationship going out with a co-worker. It's more of working with someone who reports to you over a meal … breakfast, lunch, dinner with or without drinks. Come on, you know that. The boss has the formal power. There's no power sharing."

"But there's always the possibility of a real or imagined sexual overtone if one is male and the other is female."

"Not today. Both could be the same genre." He pauses and then continues. "But the article is focusing in on what McFadden believes to be a concocted sexual harassment claim by a woman." He wiggles in his chair, feeling some built up tension in his stomach and a bit of stiffening in his neck. "I bet you hear this all the time in your company, I certainly do where I work. 'You can't go out with co-workers!' Hell, if I can't date the people I work with I'd have no friends! These are the people I know better than most others! I work with them 8 – 10 hours a week! That's what people do … they go out with people they know well! And that includes peers, subordinates and bosses … employees from the same department or from different departments, employees within the same building or within different buildings, working in the same city or in different cities! Big deal! If I didn't go out with people I work with … well … I might still be a virgin!" He takes a deep inhale of air.

"What the hell is going on with you? You're out of control!"

"I've just started." His eyes are wider than normal as he continues. "McFadden's article is making the executive, who just happens to be female, an immortal and unethical person. While I'm not saying I'd do IT for a promotion, we both know that people do it to each other to get ahead. And I mean that in the literal sense of intercourse, but come to think of it, I should mean that as well as setting someone up for failure, in a way, betrayed. But regardless, that's life! Hell, in my company we've got so much sensitivity training, H. R. policies on using the right words, ways of greeting each other with no touching. Come on, who has time for that! Everybody tells dirty jokes about the other sex, race, religion, and so on. Come on!"

She waits for him to continue, but when he doesn't she says, "You really are worked up about this. What's really going on?"

"I'm just fed up with the crap ... the politically correctness that leads to being insincere ... that doesn't solve any problems but rather makes them worse. No wonder everybody is talking about fake news. I mean ... who can anybody trust these days?" His breathing rate accelerates, but he manages to say, "Sometimes I think I'm even betraying myself."

"We've known each other for almost a year, and we don't work together, but we've never had sex. Aren't I attractive to you?"

"What?"

She leans forward just enough to emphasize the importance of her next statements. "I've been attracted to you since we first met. I was hoping you felt the same way. I guess I betrayed myself."

Whitney stays motionless throughout their conversation yet her mind is running a hundred miles an hour. She wonders who leaked the information to McFadden.

During the same day, Saunders flippantly walks into Rose's office. He nonchalantly says, "You wanted to see me, what's up?" He lets his body flop into a cushioned chair. His face is far removed from being worried looking.

Rose is quite the opposite. His face is grave, terse looking. "Sit down, it's serious. Your father-in-law has had a heart attack that has hospitalized him. His condition is critical."

Saunders straightens his body while still seated in the chair, yet his voice appears to be distant sounding. "That's terrible."

"You didn't know? Lisa didn't say anything to you?" He pauses. "You could at least act as if it matters to you."

"What the hell does that mean?" Saunders juts his chin forward trying to intimidate Rose.

"Cut out your childishness. You owe him more than you can ever imagine."

"And who the hell are you ... so righteous and just?"

"If it wasn't for marrying his daughter, you wouldn't have had a chance with him. You should count your blessings each and every minute."

"Is that it?" Saunders stands, puts his hands on his hips. "I've got things to do."

"You don't even care what hospital he's in! You're not even thinking of visiting him!"

"Like I said, I've got things to do ... like running this outfit." He turns his body away from Rose and seems to be ready to leave.

"He's known about you and Lynda from the beginning." Rose's voice is steady and determined. "He wanted to interfere but thought you'd come to see your own stupidity and return to Lisa, just like you promised when you got married to her ... or have you forgotten?"

"You don't know what you're saying."

"Oh yes I do, and you know it."

Fred swallows deeply, and then changes the topic. "He's always been an oppressive old man, domineers every chance he can. He makes it uncomfortable and stressful for me to get my job done, always looking over my shoulder, checking my every move, second guessing me along the way. He is tyrannical and cruel. I hate him!"

"Yet, you stayed with WRS in spite of all of this."

"What was I to do? Where would I go? How would Lisa take it?"

"Please, give it up. You've been waiting for him to keel over so you could take over WRS, at least that's what you still think will happen when he passes on. Huh?"

"Of all the spiteful things you can say, that's it?"

"Oh, there's more, but now's not the time."

They stare at each other … glaring and glowering … as if it is a match of who will blink first.

Don't underestimate age … Saunders, the younger of the two flutters his right eyelid, and then opens and closes his left eye to lose the standoff.

Saunders repeats a previous comment, "I've got things to do."

Saunders is about to leave Rose's office when he hears Rose say, "And Lisa … unfortunate for you about her sexual preferences. Did you know she and Lynda were lovers?"

"You're a dirty old man! Go to hell!" Saunders stomps out of the office.

Still within hearing distance, Rose shouts out to Saunders, "Don't plan on moving into Charles's office. He's already made other plans that don't include you." He pauses.

"And it wouldn't hurt if you paid the old man a visit before he goes."

In the Hospital, Charles is in and out of reality, slurring words, skipping around with thoughts that don't make sense, sometimes lucid, most times not.

Saunders sits uncomfortably in a metal chair as far away from him as he can be, resisting the urge to get up and leave, but remains not out of respect for he really despises his father-in-law whom he considers a pompous old fart, but who controls his financial life through the business, and essentially his entire life.

Charles, lying in the Hospital bed of a private room, coughs.

Saunders makes no move to assist him in finding a tissue or even a simple glass of water that is on top of a nearby night stand.

Charles wipes his mouth with the back of his hand. "I know you're not here out of respect in the normal way, but that's neither here or there. The fact is you've come to see me, to watch me die in this place." He shrugs his shoulders. "I really don't know and even care less." He coughs again with the same lack of empathy from his son-in-law who twists nervously in the chair. Then he continues. "Lisa stopped in only briefly. I guess because she found me still alive." He coughs once again, and then goes on. "I knew your father, something you've probably didn't know. We knew each other quite well … always competing. If you think I'm a son-of-a-bitch, well, you didn't know him. He lived at the bottom of the swamp." He coughs again and then waves to Saunders to come closer. "In the bottom drawer, there's a pink of whiskey and two glasses. Pour us each a drink."

Saunders frowns, walks towards the night stand and complies. He thinks the idea is appropriate given the conditions. He waits for Charles to take the first sip, and then mimics the move. He sits in another metal chair much closer to his father-in-law.

"Like I said, your father was a real dick-head. I only allowed you to marry my daughter because you seemed to be the only man she was attracted to. But honestly, I believed she knew you'd keep your mouth shut about her propensity to women, something she never suspects even today that I know as well. She keeps quiet your unfaithfulness as long as you reciprocate in kind, a nice and tidy arrangement. A match made in hell." He doesn't try to smother a loud laugh.

Charles takes a sip of whiskey from the tumbler tightly held in his hand. "I always wanted my daughter Lisa, your wife, to think of a family when she got married, but, as I just said that wasn't going to happen. I wanted her to marry someone to give her a respectable place in society, at the upper level. But that didn't happen either. Neither of you seem interested in your 5-year old daughter. Lisa's been a very big disappointment, but not much of a surprise." He pauses. "But I still love her ... hell, she's my daughter, my adopted daughter."

Saunders isn't sure where this is going. Annoyed, he swallows the whiskey from his tumbler and pours himself another shot, purposely ignoring to offer the same in kind to his father-in-law. He glares at the old man in the Hospital bed.

"But you've stuck with her." His grin is not a happy one. "Did you know you were screwing her woman?"

Saunders' eyes pop wide open. He almost drops the tumbler.

"Yeah, Lynda whatever her name is, the woman who mysteriously died. She and Lisa were lovers." He lets out a loud laugh that almost causes the tumbler to leave his hand. "Can you believe that?"

Saunders grits his teeth. "What's your stupid point?"

Deep in his heart Charles knows he's being small and mean-spirited, but he doesn't give a rat's ass. He's been living the humiliated truth for too long.

The room goes silent.

Charles picks up where he ended. "Oh, my pardon, I guess I've offended you." He smirks and then takes another sip of whiskey.

"You don't know what you're saying. You're old, angry, and heartless." Saunders' jaw tightens.

"Have it your way if that's what makes you feel less nasty yourself." Charles pauses. "You've betrayed yourself for so long you have no idea what the truth is." He checks the empty tumbler in his hand. "Pour me another one." He nods his head towards the pint bottle on the night stand. "At least we both like the same whiskey."

Saunders obeys and adds a little more to his tumbler as well.

"Look, I'm a man too. I understand temptations. I'm not going to blab to anyone so help me ... as long as you agree to one condition."

Saunders face is frozen. "What's that?"

Charles is totally serious, "So long as you leave Whitney alone."

Saunders' face turns white. He is unable to start a question. He is dazed.

Charles closes his eyes and the tumbler slips out of his hand onto the bed sheet spilling the remains of the whiskey.

Saunders stands, finishes off the remains of his whiskey, and puts the empty tumbler atop the night stand, and without saying a word storms out of the Hospital room, neither caring one way or another if his father-in-law just died or has fallen asleep.

CHAPTER 10

It's now been nearly a month since the mysterious death of Lynda Ackerman. While both the F. B. I. and the local Police have investigated the case that include, but not limited to, many people interviewed, they are no closer to finding out who the responsible person or persons are.

Additionally, while the F. B. I. has no plausible information about WRS that Whitehead, Rose, and Saunders own, as well as their own likely questionable illegal and unethical actions, it is all too ambiguous and uncertain to bring legal action at this time.

It's as if law enforcement, in looking for the truth, grab armfuls of air, but there is nothing to hold onto.

A frequent, yet unlikely, visitor to Charles in the Hospital while he recovers from his heart attack is Whitney Danica. And during her visits, many things that she thought were true flip upside down. Their talks each morning at about the same time, as he barely eats a bland and forgetful breakfast, and she sips a double espresso, are as if they have been close friends for all their lives.

While the I.V. inserted into his body is a bothersome, Whitehead ignores the inconvenience when Whitney is with him. "I wish I had said more often to her how much I loved her, but I didn't." His eyes start to water each time he thinks of Helen, his wife. "And then she died and suddenly I was alone." His eyes move towards a nearby container of water.

"Here, I'll get that for you." Whitney leans close to the flask to grab hold and then moves it close to him for an easy suck through the straw.

He continues, "She really didn't know what my businesses were all about. I couldn't tell her … she wouldn't understand why I did what I did. She'd probably have left me if she knew, something I could never have lived with myself. But I could have told her some things, a few things, not so much that she'd disrespect me, but just enough." His eyes widen as if to ask Whitney if she understands.

"I don't think I've ever been that much in love. And love, I guess, makes all the difference between two people."

His smile is more than just a friendly grin. "But you'll know it when it happens."

"I guess so." She shrugs her shoulders.

"She was walking up the street, dressed quite smartly, plaid skirt with a white silk blouse. Her hair was dark brown like dark chocolate that really accentuated her blue eyes. She was walking alone with her head down. It was mid-day if I remember. But it was so long ago." He takes in a deep breath of air and then exhales as his eyes shift to his hands crossed on top of his belly. "I remember saying to myself, 'there she is, the girl of my dreams, the one I'm going to marry.'"

"You fell in love just like that?"

"I was young, but not dumb. I knew it when I saw her and felt it in my heart."

"Remarkable." Whitney takes another sip of espresso.

"And then what?" Her eyes are as bright and inquisitive as can be.

"I figured she was about my age, a few years younger if I had to guess. I was still in high school, but the school was a large public school that she could have been a student there as well. That didn't matter to me. I was going ask her to a dance at school."

"So you didn't know her, you had never seen her before, is that what you're saying?"

"Exactly." He pauses to think of something. "I'll never forget the rush of emotions that I felt through my body. It was like I couldn't move or think straight, but I knew she was the real deal for me. So, I shoved my hands in my pockets, looked at the beautiful girl who I was going to ask out for a date, and nodded to myself. I stepped towards her, introduced myself, and then I blurted out something. I don't know what I said, but she giggled and said yes." His eyes shine brightly as if he had just experienced it for the first time. He looks away, his eyes get dim, and he starts to tear.

Whitney feels herself get choked up. She grabs a tissue, leans towards him to dry out his eyes. She doesn't know what to say, so she decides to stay quiet.

The touch of Whitney's hands brings him out of his self-imposed daze. He quickly changes the subject. "I'm a superstitious person, always have been. I wear this medal around my neck." He pulls a chain from around his neck to expose a religious image. "See, I can't ever remember not wearing it." He hesitates and then continues, "I'm not religious in an old-fashioned sense, like going to church or anything like that, but I'm superstitious. I feel comfortable with repetition and customs, you know like habits and rituals." His eyes seek an acknowledgement from her.

Whitney nods, "Sure. I understand. Me too ... in some ways."

He shakes his head sideways. "I'm rambling on." He thinks twice before continuing.

"No, no, please. I want to hear more, but only if you want to. But I do, I really do." Her eyes beg him to carry on.

"OK, if it's alright with you."

Her enthusiastic nods are convincing.

"I feel quite comfortable talking with you. You're a good listener." His voice seems to have changed to something more serious and important.

She blushes without saying a word, not realizing what he's about to say and the severe sounding tone he'll use.

His voice is completely serious sounding, "I've learned from my business dealings to be careful who to trust."

Her mouth gapes open, surprised at what she hears and the danger she thinks it implies.

He continues in the same vein. "It's rare to find someone you can confide in, even rarer to find a friend. I couldn't imagine having a better business partner than Hank Rose. We share common values and we stick strictly to whatever the business is at hand. You wash my back and I wash yours ... you understand." All of a sudden he looks at her with laser like eyes.

Whitney feels an upsurge in emotion ... the feeling that you get when someone is revealing something critically important. She nods her head in agreement and almost loosens her grip on the coffee cup.

"That's called loyalty and respect ... that's a special

trust ... no betrayal ... but power. It's about getting and keeping power. And when you're poor, regardless of whether it's economic, emotional, spiritual, or whatever, with nothing like I once was as a young boy, you look up to those who have the power. That's something I'll never forget." He looks away, just over her head at the wall, and then wraps his eyes around hers. "And then, of course, there is revenge ... to get even with those who have betrayed you."

Whitney feels her heart tighten, almost to a level of pain. She does all she can to catch her breath.

He closes his eyes and leans back into bed. "I feel tired. So sorry, but I need to rest."

Pleased that he's given her an out to leave at this time, she carefully plans her words, "I've taken too much of your time. Can I come back tomorrow morning?"

Still with his eyes closed, he smiles in a cheery manner. "I hope so. I enjoy WRS." His voice is calm, and he sounds pleased.

This will be the last time she will see him alive.

The next day Rose and Whitney privately talk in his office.

"He died peacefully late last night. I'm going to miss him badly." He pauses, tilts his head downward as a whisper of moisture appears in his eyes. He rubs away the moisture. "I couldn't imagine having a better friend and business partner than him. That's how great deals are done ... with someone you trust ... who's got your back ... both ways. Even when we weren't doing business together back in the day, we talked almost every day. And that's how he felt about you. I've got to show you something that he wanted me to do if he couldn't do it himself."

He steps away from his chair to unlock a drawer at the bottom of his desk. It is a package about the size of an 8 ½ X 11 inch picture frame. He hands it to her. "Please open it and I'll describe what you see."

Whitney takes the package in her hand but appears hesitant to discover its contents.

"Go ahead, please unwrap it." His voice is peaceful and soothing to her ears.

Slowly she unwraps the package until she has a full view of it. Her eyes are glued to the photograph.

"He wanted you to have that."

Whitney looks up, not sure the importance of the apparent family photo she holds in her hands. Her mouth opens but there is no sound.

"When we both first met you, under rather tense conditions … I'm sure you remember … we both knew or should I say he knew while I suspected who you were." He chuckles a little and then continues. "We did D.N.A. on you that resulted in what Charles believed to be true, proving that you are his daughter who was given up for adoption. He and Helen believed they didn't have the means to provide a good family life for you. But later on, they adopted Lisa, who turned out to be a real prima donna. They had no idea where you were."

Whitney isn't sure where she is at the moment. It seems her life has flashed back and forth in record speed. She feels slightly dizzy. Her eyes look unsteady. She is not able to speak.

Rose quickly moves closer to her, arm now wrapped

around her shoulder to steady her body. "I know this is all a surprise. He would have told you had he lived longer. He told me each day you were with him in the Hospital how much he enjoyed your closeness. He really loved you, but at the same time never forgave himself for putting you up for adoption. It broke his heart as well as his wife's. When she passed away he committed to finding you, but was not successful. And then you surprised him, one of the greatest, if not the greatest gift he could have received."

Whitney suddenly breaks down in tears, crying like a child in an uncontrolled manner.

Rose wraps both arms around her for comfort. "I know he's in a good place smiling at you with all his love."

She looks up at Rose, eyes fully soaked with tears. She sniffles and then says, "I can feel him without touching him. I can see him with my eyes closed. I can even smell the aroma of his skin. His voice is clear to me in spite of him not being here. And I will think of him always."

"Yes, I understand." Rose pauses and then continues with other important news. "And now there is something else you need to know … something very important that Charles would have told you himself if he could."

Whitney's eyes pop open very wide.

"He chose you to replace himself as C. E. O. of WRS, and the paperwork is complete. All that is needed is your signature. It takes place immediately." He stares at her for a reaction.

She puts her hands over her mouth but is able to squeeze out something, "No way."

Rose nods affirmatively, "It is what he wanted, and he told me how proud he was of you. Also, I'll be by your side all the while. There are a few things we'll need to talk about, to get you up-to-date, but nothing to worry about." He frowns, "You're not thinking about declining this once in a lifetime opportunity, are you?"

"I – I don't know what to say. It's all so sudden."

"Get used to it. This is a fast paced business, and you'll have to make important decisions with sometimes not as much information as you'd like, or enough time. But that's what it is … that's the reality of business in today's fast paced and rapidly changing global world. Charles believed you were up to it, but more importantly, do you believe you are?" He holds her eyes glued to his. "What's your decision?"

"What about Fred? I mean, he's gonna be pissed, really pissed."

"Of course, but somebody's always going to get pissed about something, some decision they don't agree with, whether it rains when they want sun, whether the traffic moves as fast as they want. It's life. The key is to get on with it. The human body is not made to coast … it's made to move forward, to stay in motion, to advance your agenda."

"Who's gonna tell him?"

"That's easy."

"And … ?"

"Together we tell him."

"He won't like it."

"Haven't you been listening to me? He isn't going to like it. One, he's always figured he was next in line. That, by the way is utter bull shit, but that's what he thought. Two, he's going to be angry at you, thinking you stole something that belonged to him. That two is bull shit. Three … this will probably be the most difficult for him to come to grips with, he'll have to face his wife, Charles' adopted daughter. She's going to flip. She'll never come to grips with the decision thinking she was going to be the wife of the C. E. O.. Oh yeah, they won't like it one bit."

"So what do we do?" Whitney sounds unsure.

"For you … stop worrying about something you can't control. Do what you want to do. If you don't want the job, then tell me." He eyes are abnormally wide, verging on being angry. "What the hell do you want?"

Whitney swallows a few times, takes in a few breaths of air, and then eventually dares to look him squarely in the eyes. "OK, show me the paperwork, I'm in."

"No turning back. Once you're in, you're in."

"You've already said that, and I heard it loud and clear. I'm ready to take life directly on."

Rose steps to his desk where there is a folder containing several documents. "Here it is, all prepared for your signature. Come on over. I'll show you where to sign and date."

She feels her heartbeat pick up, to her a positive sign of confidence and high spirits. She finishes the signage in less than three minutes.

"Congratulations, Ms. C. E. O.." Rose extends his hand to shake.

She prefers to grab hold of him for a hug. Then, with her two arms tightly clenched around his shoulders, she quietly says, "Thank you for your confidence in me. I'll not let you down," as she looks upward. A tear trickles down her cheek.

Rose waits for a signal to release his arms around his new boss.

She drops her hands and then steps back one pace from

him. "I'll be counting on you all the way." She looks upward, "And to you, father, I'll make you proud."

Rose waits until she's through, and then says, "I suggest the first order of business is to talk with Fred."

"I agree."

"Maybe we should think though the game plan ... you know ... what you'll say, what I may say, what he'll probably say."

"Agreed."

"He's going to be surprised."

"I'd say more like shocked."

Rose chuckles, "Yes, but that won't stop him from babbling about all sorts of things."

"We'll let him vent, rant, and rave. Then, after he flushes out his rage, what next?"

"You have the authority to continue his current contract with the organization that expires in nine months from now. You can also cancel his current contract immediately or within a few weeks from now and pay him severance."

"How much is that?"

"It's hefty. He'd get three million dollars paid out evenly over three years, along with full medical benefits for him and his family for the same duration."

Wrinkles appear on Whitney's forehead. "Wow."

"It is what it is. We've got the dough, so there's nothing financial to worry about."

"Is there a confidentiality clause?"

"Yes, we all have it. He's got to keep his trap shut for ten years about anything related to the businesses, and that includes the people we currently or in the past have worked with, customers, suppliers, employees, and so forth. It's all spelled out in the contract."

"So, even if there's something he'd want to tell, to whomever, even law enforcement, he can't, is that what I hear you saying?"

"Precisely ... even law enforcement, but deals are often made under full immunity. That's something out of our control. Now, there's nothing we've done in the past, are doing now, or plan on doing in the future that violated, is violating, or would violate a law of any kind." He grins ever so slightly but just enough for Whitney to pick up on.

She nods her head, "That's good to hear." She pauses, "What if he wants another position within the company?"

"That would totally be your decision, but I'd recommend against it."

"What do you recommend?"

"We pay him his severance, and say goodbye."

"I agree."

"You'll have to think of a replacement for him. The President's role could be very helpful to you, regardless of whether the person is an insider or someone from outside the Company. I probably know the job better than you and could serve as a sort of mentor, even if you decided to change the nature of the job."

"Do I call you Hank, Rose, Chief Legal Counsel, or something else?"

"Whatever pleases you is fine with me."

"OK, Hank it is." She smiles. "The person who I've trusted the most is someone named Karen O'Leary. She's the one currently responsible for the Company Blog, is very competent, easy to work with, and can be trusted. She respects me and vice-versa."

"Sounds like an excellent profile."

"OK, she's the one I want to be our next President, and she'll continue control over the Company Blog. We can find someone else in the Company to replace her for the other responsibilities she currently has. I know someone who's studying stuff in college who might be a good addition, although he's not currently an employee with us. But Karen could easily mentor him. He's a good guy."

"As long as you trust him … that's very important."

Whitney takes in another breath of air and then lets it out. She says, "Definitely." She pauses and then continues, "I think I'm ready to talk with Fred."

"I'll set up the appointment right now. Don't go anywhere."

Whitney suddenly remembers something. "Oh, one last question."

Rose turns to face her, "Yes?"

"Did he ever mention to you about implanting an R.F.I.D. chip in me?"

He frowns and then shakes his head. "Not that I recall, but it wouldn't surprise me. Charles was a very unique man. Why are you asking?"

"One had been implanted in me but was inoperative. I had it removed a little while ago."

"Oh." He shrugs his shoulders as if to brush off the topic.

She isn't sure what to think about his reaction, but for the time being, returns to the previous topic. "I'm ready to talk with Fred."

"There's no way I'm leaving without a fight!" Fred is outraged. He knew something was up when Rose called him for an emergency meeting, and felt it was a matter of life or death, but not his own. He wonders if there is any chance for a clean getaway from his past.

"It's all here, signed and dated by your father-in-law before he died. Did you ever join your wife when she went to the Hospital when she was notified?" Rose is enjoying the mockery. "Remember this is being recorded."

He ignores Rose's last comment. "Of course I was there!" He lies and Rose knows he's lying.

Rose continues, "You'll let me know of the funeral arrangements so we can notify the employees and business associates of your father-in-law?"

"Go to hell!"

"Have it your way." Rose glances towards Whitney. "As previously stated, the new C. E. O. will be announcing the reorganization soon. It is probably in your best interest not to be around since it most likely will be uncomfortable for you, especially when the new President is introduced."

"Screw you!"

Whitney remains silent as recommended by Rose, a good idea she tells herself at the present time. She continues to listen and watch.

Fred glares at Whitney, "You're not going to get away with this. I know things about you that you don't want shared." He feels his breathing rate increase. "You bitch!"

Rose continues with a calm and unruffled sounding voice. "I interpret that as a threat against her. I'm a witness to this conversation, and again, to remind you a third time, this is being recorded."

"Screw it all! This isn't over!"

"So, you're not going to sign the paperwork?" Rose asks.

"What do you think, you shit head?"

"As the Chief Legal Counsel of WRS, I suggest you reconsider."

Fred flips him the middle finger of his right hand, turns and leaves Rose and Whitney together.

She says, "Well, that didn't go very well." She isn't sure whether to grin or growl.

"Actually, it went better than I thought it would go. Right after I contacted him and therefore immediately before this meeting I notified Security that Fred Saunders, the former President, would be leaving the Company, but to be on alert in case we needed them to assist. I think it's time now that I instruct them to go to his office to make sure he leaves the building once and for all with only his personal effects, nothing related to the Company. I would normally contact H. R. but we both know who's in charge there."

"Yes, I've been thinking of a replacement for him as well. He's useless and I wonder how on earth he ever was appointed to the job. Care to enlighten me?"

"Fred pushed for it. Charles didn't care. I was outnumbered." Rose shrugs his shoulders, "Which reminds me." He pauses and then continues, "If you agree, I should announce to the Company the death of our former C. E. O., the realignment of the executives, and then we'll contact our P.R. firm to broadcast it to the media."

"You're thinking of everything." She grins. "I'm fortunate not to go this alone."

"That's why you're paying me the big bucks … and it's the way Charles would have wanted it."

"So, it's time you contact Security," she reminds him. "And let's talk with Samuelson together soon. He might be useful to us in some capacity." She shrugs her shoulders not exactly sure what role he might be suitable for.

Rose nods approvingly, "I understand. Excuse me while I make the call." He reaches for his cell to notify Security.

In his office, alone for the time being, Fred Saunders is on the phone talking with his wife. "That's right! They canned me! It's immediate!"

Outraged but not surprised, Lisa says, "She probably gave him a blow job before he died!" She pauses. "What are you going to do?"

"There's nothing I can do, at least legally. The paperwork is legit and with Rose involved it would definitely hold up if challenged."

"So you're going to crawl away on your stomach!"

"I too don't like the sound of that, but what other choice do I have?"

"You know things that they don't want told!"

"And they know things that we don't want told … it's a stalemate. I think I'm going to take the money and walk away."

"You're really that fragile … my, oh my."

While her biting comment was expected by him, he has no come back to give. His shoulders droop as if he just barely finished a fifteen round heavyweight boxing match that he lost. He's worn out. His head hangs down.

Lisa yells, "Are you still there?"

The sound of her piercing voice brings him back. "Yeah, I'm still here."

"And what do I tell my friends? That my husband got fired by an immoral, promiscuous, loose, and unrestrained bitch? Is that what I'm supposed to say? Huh?"

"Say whatever you want to say. But also remember the secrets you've kept hidden and how easily they can sneak out."

"What the hell are you talking about?"

"For one, do I have to mention HER name and what happened to HER?"

"What are you saying?"

"You know what I'm saying, you and Lynda Ackerman. Did you think I didn't know about you and her, and what many suspect about her mysterious death? Please."

"How dare you accuse me of ... !" The shriek of her voice is quickly weakened. There is a long pause when neither person talks. Then Lisa sniffles, "So sad, too bad."

"What are you saying? Did you ...?" He's not able to finish the question. It's as if he has been kicked in the teeth from out of the blue.

She tries to change the subject to him. "And it's not as if she and you were a secret!"

"What are you implying?"

"I'm not implying anything! I'm stating a fact well known by many people ... my friends among others! But I kept it a hush-hush to protect our marriage ... to protect you!"

"And you!"

"You've always had delusions ... you're mostly

inadequate. And you've never seemed to cause others to be happy wherever you go, only when they go and leave you."

Suddenly there is silence. Then he hears the phone disconnect. Finally there is a knock on his closed door.

His name is called out. "Mr. Saunders, we're from Security. Can we come in?"

He keeps his back to the closed door. Resigned to his fate he answers but the sound of his voice is weak. "Yeah sure, come on in."

The door opens.

He turns to see two uniformed Security Guards standing at the opened door to his office. One guard says, "We've been directed to help you pack your personal effects, cancel your passwords and codes, and escort you out of the building."

Rose and Whitney finish up the paperwork to confirm her promotion to C. E. O..

"That should do it. This is yours." He hands to her a copy of the documents.

There is a moment of silence.

"I'd like for the both of us to talk with Karen O'Leary together. Let's do that now."

"Here or in her office?"

"Well, she's currently in an open space, so it might be better here. I'll call her now." She waits for Rose's non-verbal acknowledgement and then she dials.

"Karen, it's me. Can you come to my office … I mean the C. E. O.'s office now. There's something good to tell you." She listens for a second and then adds, "No, it's all good, I promise." Whitney hangs up the phone and looks at Rose. "She thought maybe she did something wrong. Can you imagine how she's going to react when we tell her?"

In less than five minutes later, Karen sits in a comfortable chair in the C. E. O.'s office. She looks around to see Whitney and Rose smiling. She's confused. "Where's Mr. Whitehead?"

Whitney motions to Rose to make the announcement. "He died late last night from heart complications."

Karen covers her mouth with an opened hand, "Oh, I'm so sorry. I didn't know he had been ill." She looks at Whitney and then back to Rose. "What is it that you want me to do?" Her face is sad looking.

Whitney's voice is cheerful. "I want you to accept a promotion to President of WRS. Will you accept?"

Karen is temporarily stunned. Her hand returns to cover her mouth. She is speechless.

Whitney continues. "That's right. We want you to be the new President and join me since … I'm the new C. E. O.!" Her head nods nonstop for several seconds, and her eyes are popped wide open. "That's right, you heard me. I'm the new C. E. O., and we want you to be the new President!"

First comes shock, then it is followed by denial, and finally there is acceptance. "You're serious about this, aren't you?"

She is quick to confirm, "Quite serious." Whitney's voice mimics the affirmation. "The three of us are going to be a great team!"

"Yes! I'm all in!" Karen quickly stands to grab hold of Whitney for a hug. She starts to cry.

Rose steps back a ways to witness their joint celebration. He stays quiet.

Whitney eyes Rose a few feet away. "Get over here. We're in this together."

Rose takes pleasure in joining the two women.

A few seconds pass without anyone speaking. Then Karen asks, "How did this all happen?"

Whitney decides now isn't the time to get into the details. "We'll talk about that at a later time. But now, it's the three of us. Saunders has left the Company."

Karen, who is still overwhelmed by the unexpected professional upgrade, sniffles and then says, "I guess this is where the phrase …." She starts to cry again, unable to finish her thought.

Both Whitney and Rose realize that Karen's got to get the emotion out of her system, so they look at her as would a mother and father fondly watching their daughter revel.

The short time in celebration passes at a snail's pace for both Whitney and Rose. Rose and Whitney look at each other at the same time. There are more priorities they have to attend to.

Whitney starts it off, "sorry to break up the mood, but there are some loose ends that need attention." She looks at Karen, "For the moment, keep all of this quiet until we tell you otherwise. Hank and I have a few more related issues to tidy up. How do you feel about our H. R. guy, Samuelson?"

Karen wastes no time. "He's worthless."

Rose grins as Whitney continues, "No surprise. We

agree. But he might just come around if we give him one last chance."

Rose adds as he looks at Karen, "Whoever is the H. R. Director will report to you."

Karen takes in a deep breath of air through her nose and then lets it flow out of her mouth. "Well, everybody deserves a second chance, I guess." She pauses and then continues, "OK, let's keep him on, but I'll have a short leash around his fat neck."

Whitney nods, "Agreed." She looks at Rose, "Maybe you should call him to your office with the three of us present. Nothing like a good surprise to get the point that there's new leadership in town."

Ten minutes later as Rose, Whitney, and Karen sit in Rose's office there is a knock on the door.

Rose shouts out, "Come in."

As soon as Samuelson steps into the office he suddenly realizes something big is up. His attention is as striking as a lightning bolt. His swallow is deep, and his cough is as coarse as sandpaper. He suddenly hears nothing, only seeing their lips move. Then he snaps out of the self-induced daze when he hears Rose say, "Have a seat." He moves slowly towards an empty chair. He tells himself he'd prefer to return to the spell he was just in rather than to face them, but he really has no choice in the matter. He takes another needed gulp of air to help settle down.

"Good morning Sheldon," says Rose. His voice is polite yet with a sliver of danger.

Samuelson is disconcerted at the sound of his first name

being mentioned, something that's been uncommon during his employment with the Company. Yet, he manages to answer, "Yes, good morning Mr. Rose." He coughs and then finds a lane in the conversation to acknowledge the two women who are currently quiet, "and to you as well, Miss Danica and Miss O'Leary." He knows he's really screwing up the talk but under the present conditions he's at least happy he's able to say anything.

Rose continues. "There's been an unfortunate situation in the Company."

Samuelson now believes this is when the ax will fall on him. All he is able to do is swallow a few dribbles of saliva, but the feeling isn't good.

Rose takes up again. "Charles Whitehead has passed away." He waits no time to get on with the next statement. "And according to Mr. Whitehead's wish, Miss Danica is now our C. E. O., and Miss O'Leary has been promoted to be our new President. Mr. Saunders has stepped down." Now is the time for Rose to watch Samuelson squirm, something to enjoy. He waits a short time enjoying the pleasure of Samuelson's uncomfortableness, and then continues. "This leads to your role as H. R. Director." Again, there is another purposeful pause to take in his creepy amusement. "Would you like to stay employed with WRS with Miss O'Leary as your new boss?" His smile is an odd looking grin, more of a sneer than anything else.

The room goes silent for a few seconds, and then Samuelson lets out a loud fart.

Rose laughs, "I don't quite understand that … is that to mean a yes or no?"

Samuelson finds a way to compose himself yet he notices the two women snicker. "I – I'd like to stay on."

Now's the time for Karen to speak, "OK, that's fine with me. I look forward to working with you."

Her answer, while clearly stated, is not believed by anyone in the room. It is what it is, and everyone wonders how long his employment status will last.

Karen steps up in the conversation. "I'm going to be blunt with you. We've never been on the same page since your, ah promotion, to H. R. Director. I attributed that to you being new in the job … lots of things to learn and, let's be honest, a very high profile position. Agreed?"

"Ye – yes, I suppose so."

"Sheldon, you either believe or you don't believe. Which is it?"

"Ye – yes, I agree. I believe that." He clears his throat. His mind temporarily wanders off someplace not well known even to him.

"I've got to count on you for one hundred percent. The first meeting you had with the employees was a joke. You didn't seem prepared in spite of some crappy cheat sheets in your hand. Maybe you need some professional training in presentation making, and even professional H. R. such as staffing, recruiting, total compensation, employee relations, safety and employment law, just to mention a few areas. What do you think about that?"

"Yes, that would be great. Yes, oh yes."

"There's got to be a local chapter for H. R. professionals. Almost every business specialty has one. Find out what it is, join it, and start taking some workshops."

"Yes, I'll get on it immediately."

"And one more thing while I'm thinking of ways to improve yourself." Karen pauses. "This is very important, so listen." She quickly looks at Whitney and then at Rose before returning her eyes to him. She scans his body as if inspecting a piece of machinery. "Drop at least fifteen pounds. You're overweight and most likely prone to illness. I can't have someone who isn't one hundred percent fit to work."

His eyeballs widen and then freeze in place. He can't believe what he's just heard, and is about to object to her assessment when all of a sudden he lets out another loud fart. His face turns red as he drops his head toward the floor. He decides now is not the time to confront his boss, maybe at another time, maybe never. He meekly swallows saliva along with his pride.

The room returns to stillness. Everyone is speechless until his voice makes an audible noise. "Yes, I agree."

Whitney decides it's time to end the meeting, thinking the main purpose has been covered. "Alright then, thanks for coming in Sheldon. Welcome to the new alignment. I'm happy to know that we can count on you." Her lukewarm smile signifies for him to leave.

Samuelson nods a tidy bit, stands, and leaves the trio alone.

As Samuelson slowly walks away he decides to take the stairs rather than the elevator. He wants time to think about it all and not have to deal with another human being for a while, especially if that human being is an employee.

By the time he reaches his office, he hesitates to rethink

the decision to make a call. He's got to have all his ducks in order. He wipes his mouth with the palm of his left hand. His right foot begins to uncontrollably stomp the floor indicating he's about to lose control so he grabs hold of the edge of his desk to steady himself.

On top of his bargain basement priced desk rests a framed picture of a woman he doesn't even know. She smiles although she too doesn't know him. It's one of many picture frames he's bought over the years just for the pictures of the women that the frames contained. Weird in a way, that it gives him some sort of comfort just looking at the picture of someone he doesn't even know.

Now that he's settled down, he lets his body flop on the matching shoddy chair. Then he goes for it … he reaches for his cell to call someone. Within two rings he hears her voice.

Carol McFadden looks at caller I.D. and then says, "Well, well Sheldon. Do you have something juicy for me again? I'm all ears."

Fifteen minutes later, Samuelson finally disconnects the phone, hoping he had made a favorable impression with her, the second time he's talked with her. He checks his watch … noon … lunch time.

He slowly walks out of his office, more like a waddle, as his upper body leans back and forth to the sides with each step. He's already forgotten about his commitment to lose weight.

Before he realizes it, he's at the cafeteria line for lunch. He's got the menu memorized. He's almost immune to the stares from others, but not completely. Their eyes, at first are of surprise, and then turn to a funny look. At times he believes hearing them call him 'fatty,' just like when he was in grade school.

His weight has always been a problem for as far back as he can remember … uncontrollable eating linked with the unhealthiest of foods imaginable. He used to be ashamed, but over time he found a way to betray himself, yet he cannot remember a time when he felt totally comfortable with his situation and socially with his classmates. He tended to avoid attending any events that were voluntary. And, come to think of it, he never had a 'best friend.'

At work, he's actually turned down promotional opportunities that would have put him physically in contact with others. However, the promotion to H. R. Director this time was too much of a good deal to turn away, in spite of knowing he'd feel the same way as when he was younger when he would unnecessarily expose himself to being teased by others.

He makes his luncheon selection in an almost robotic way, eager to find a table someplace hidden in the corner of the cafeteria away from others so that he won't have to interact with anyone. This time, he also wants to think through the recent call to McFadden, although there isn't any turning back. It is what it is.

Still in Rose's office, Karen looks at Whitney and Rose. "He's a total flunky."

Rose adds, "But he's the flunky we know. Better to know the person we're working with than not know someone that we work with."

The conversation veers Whitney's thinking to someone else. "I know a guy currently in B-School who might be a good backup."

Rose asks, "Someone you trust?"

She grins, "Oh yeah, definitely so."

Karen asks, "Someone we might know?"

"Not probable, but still someone I think you'd both like."

Rose asks, "Does he currently work in H. R.?"

"I'd say in an ancillary profession. He knows to keep quiet about sensitive things."

Karen tilts her head slightly upward with curiosity. "You've worked with him before?"

"You could say that."

Karen asks, "And he and I would get along well?"

"I couldn't image that not happening."

Rose adds, "You might casually ask him about it, you know, pass along the idea to him when you see him next. No hurry."

Whitney agrees, "I just might do that."

Suddenly Rose's cell rings. He looks at caller I.D. and then his eyebrows rise so they become curved and high, "Interesting." He looks at Whitney, "Seems Fred wants to talk." Rose smiles as he connects, "Hello Fred." He listens for less than a minute. "Sure, that's possible, but I'll need to pass it by Whitney for approval." He listens more. "No, I don't think she'll have any problems, but she is the C. E. O. and I work for her. You understand." He listens again. "Let's agree to meet at the Club tomorrow for lunch, say at one. I'll notify them." He listens again. "I'll ask her, but she's quite busy these days and she might not be able to change her schedule. But I'll tell her you asked." He listens some more. "Fine. Great. See you tomorrow at one at the Club. Have a good day." He disconnects the cell and then turns to face Whitney. "Fred Saunders has agreed to voluntarily resign with the same terms and conditions we previously talked about with him. I guess he came to his senses. He wanted to know if you would be present at tomorrow's lunch, and you heard my answer. Quite honestly, Whitney, I don't think it's worth your time."

Whitney nods in agreement. "Agreed, thanks for working this out amicably for everyone."

After Fred hangs up, he hesitates to look at his wife, Lisa, who has been listening to his part of the conversation with Rose. He has her image vividly in his head already ... jutted out jaw, lips tightly pinched, and eyes that glare into his entire body. Slowly and without enthusiasm he tilts his eyes to meet hers.

She wastes no time in expressing her displeasure. "You're a pathetic excuse for a man!" She shakes her head sideways a few times, increasingly unsettled with his shameful behavior. "You're despicable!"

There comes a time in one's life ... that's not to say there couldn't be several times in one's life ... when you've had enough. This is such a time. "Listen to me! You're reprehensible! You don't even try to be a mother to our five year old daughter as I work my ass off to pay for your flight of imagination material needs. You somehow think that a paid illegal alien nanny will do the job but all she does, it seems, is to care more about feeding her fat face and watch television reruns than care for our daughter, while you cheat on your husband with another woman pretending to be socially responsible to whatever fancies you at the moment. Your sensible causes, as you call them, change so fast you forget about the last one as soon as you find a new one. I should never have married you in the first place."

Lisa keeps still during his tantrum, thinking he'll eventually run out of gas as he normally does. The wait is not long as silence envelops both of them. Then she asks with as polite and sweet of a voice she can come up with. "Are you done, dear? Do you feel better?"

Not surprised, he has one last comment before he turns and walks away, "You fucking whore!"

"Keep in mind I know what you, Whitehead, and Rose have been up to all these years. I'm not dumb and I don't think you'd want law enforcement to know."

He stops and then turns to face her. "What are you talking about?"

"Please. I'd hate to have to dredge up so many shady and unpleasant incidents from the past."

"You don't know what you're saying." He turns around once again to leave her alone inside their house.

Standing outside their house, Fred still feels his nerves as if they are pins and needles pricking his entire body. He wiggles his shoulders to try to rid of the irritation, but the more he moves the angrier he becomes. He's got to find a way to get even with her for all the years she's tormented him. Then suddenly something comes to mind. He hesitates for only a brief moment before he punches a number on his cell. He nervously waits for an answer.

"Detective Burns. How can I help you?"

"You might not remember me but we talked a little while ago." The sound of his voice reflects his physical and emotional condition … scratchy and burning. "I'm Fred Saunders."

Burns' eyes widen with an assortment of surprise and delight. He clearly remembers him but needs to keep the jubilance undercover for a while. "Oh, let me see … oh yes, I remember our conversation, something about a death of a young woman. Was that it?"

Fred feels a wee-bit settled. "Yes, her name was Lynda Ackerman."

"That's right, I remember now."

"You interviewed me, although I remember it more as an interrogation."

"Mr. Saunders, that's how we do things."

"Have you found out the cause of her death?"

"With all due respect, Mr. Saunders, that's official law enforcement information that I can't discuss with you."

"Oh, well, I might have some new information that might help you."

While Burns takes pleasure in being brought up to date he won't let on how much he relishes the news. His voice remains composed. "And what might that be?"

"I know who killed the woman."

This isn't exactly what he was expecting to hear. He almost loses his composure but quickly recovers, "Who?"

His answer is straightforward without mincing any words, "My wife."

Burns can't believe the unequivocal response. He swallows quickly, "Your wife? Is that what you said?"

"Yes it is."

"How do know your wife killed Lynda Ackerman?"

Burns' response is immediate, "She told me."

"Straight out?"

He lies, "Yes."

"And you believe her?"

"Absolutely."

"Where is she now?"

"Inside the house."

"Is she alone?"

"Yes, our daughter is with the nanny."

"And where are you now?"

"Outside the house in the driveway."

"Don't leave. Stay right where you are. Don't go inside the house. If she starts to leave the house, call me immediately. What's the address?"

"130 Pagewood Place in the Meadows Community."

"I know exactly where you are. They'll be a clearly marked police car in ten minutes. They'll identify themselves. I'll be there in about twenty minutes."

"OK."

"Are you sure you're alright?"

"I feel great."

The phones disconnect.

As Fred Saunders and Detective Burns finish their conversation, inside the house something else unexpectedly happens. Lisa's cell phone buzzes.

She looks at the incoming call number, it is unknown. She considers ignoring the call but something prompts her to pick up. "Hello?"

"Is this Lisa Saunders?"

She doesn't recognize the voice. About to hang up the caller provides further information.

"I'm Whitney Danica."

Lisa's body temperature quickly starts to rise, prepared to hang up or else give Whitney a verbal dressing-down that she'll never forget. Yet, for some reason she does neither. "Yes?"

"Am I speaking with Lisa Saunders?"

Lisa's temperament returns to normal. "Who the hell did you expect?"

"I'd like to talk with you about something mutual between us. Is now a good time?"

"How did you get this number?"

"Fred has you listed as his emergency contact."

She yells at Whitney, "Well, you can delete that information since he's no longer working with WRS, thanks to you."

Whitney calculates her response, "That's something between your husband and the Company."

Lisa is further ticked off. "Who the hell do you think you are firing my husband? If it wasn't for him, the Company would be nothing!" She pauses. "And you'll even probably change the name of the Company as well to completely get rid of him ... and me!"

"I didn't call you to talk about that. It's something else."

Lisa is curious, "Really?" While she is more interested in hauling Whitney over hot coals, she listens. "Go on."

"It's about the late Charles Whitehead, you and me."

Lisa is cautious in wanting to get into that topic, but her curiosity outweighs the self-alert. "Oh?"

"We both know you're his daughter … adopted daughter by his wife Helen and him, but did you know that I'm his biological daughter … given up for adoption at an age I don't ever remember."

Lisa stays quiet and then says, "Oh?"

"Did you know that?"

Lisa clears her throat, somehow thinking there's a hook about to take hold of her body. "No."

Whitney's voice is slightly quivering, "What I'm saying is that we're sisters."

Lisa can't hold it in any longer. She lets loose. "So my sister fired my husband so she could run the entire Company!" She briefly halts talking and then starts up again. "And who knows what special services you gave to your father and maybe even Rose to get the job!"

Whitney is taken aback, not entirely knocked out cold, but certainly stunned. "You're quite a piece of work."

Lisa is about to go woman to woman … head to head … with Whitney, but all of a sudden she hears a strange noise outside the house. She walks towards the front window to take a peek at what's causing the sound. She sees a clearly marked police car pull in the driveway with one man and one woman both dressed in police uniforms inside the vehicle. A minute or so of conversation between Fred and the police officers ensues and then Fred motions towards the house with his head.

Lisa drops the cell phone on the floor, still connected with Whitney, and freezes in place. She continues to stare through the window as the police officers and Fred seem to continue talking about something she doesn't know for certain, but definitely would like to know for sure.

Ten minutes later, a black four door unmarked vehicle settles in behind the marked police car. Lisa does not recognize the driver at first, still stunned from what's going on.

Outside, Burns gets out of his car to walk towards Fred for a few seconds of talk. The police officers step a few feet away, but close enough to overhear their conversation. Then Burns says to Fred, "Open the door. I'll follow you. Let's make this as simple as possible."

Both men walk into the house.

Lisa remains motionless in the same spot she dropped her cell that remains connected allowing Whitney to listen in. In spite of everything, Lisa does her best to look unruffled, but inside her body there is turbulence.

Fred is the first to speak. "Lisa, this is Detective Burns. He has something to say to you."

While Lisa glances between her husband and Burns, she immediately recognizes the Detective, frowns with anger and says, "I know who he is." Then she places a stare at Burns, "Or perhaps you've forgotten?"

Lisa then remains quiet as Burns ignores her sarcasm but quickly says, "Mrs. Saunders, I need you to come downtown to the Precinct to answer a few questions about Miss Lynda Ackerman."

Lisa snaps to consciousness as if nothing unusual just took place. "I've already told you everything I know, or have you forgotten."

Burns is persistent, "Just a few loose ends. It shouldn't take much time."

Lisa gives Fred a dirty look. "What the hell have you said?"

Fred shrugs his shoulders without comment, but clearly with a smug grin.

Burns steps forward towards Lisa, "I think it's time we talk some more."

"I'm not going anyplace unless I am legally represented!" She looks at Fred for help. "Huh?"

Fred wryly responds. "That's up to you. I can't help you this time. You're on your own."

She stares angrily at her husband. It isn't only hatred that keeps her quiet at this time because that could be too easily broken by itself. It is the thought of revenge that she really feels. She'll settle the score one way or another, but that all depends on how long each of them lives.

Burns steps closer to Lisa, grabs her arm, and says, "You have the right to remain silent. Anything you say …." He takes her into custody leaving Fred alone in the house.

Lisa doesn't hear the rest of the Miranda Rights. Her brain has temporarily shut down.

Still alone in his house, Fred notices Lisa's phone on the floor. As he reaches for it he notices it is still connected to whomever his wife was talking to just before. He speaks into the phone, "Who's there?" All he hears is a click that indicates a disconnection. He tosses the phone on a nearby chair, and then decides he just might follow Burns to the Precinct in case he's needed. But before he leaves his house he calls Rose.

Whitney, on the other hand, has a hard time processing what she's heard on the phone. 'Does Lisa have information about Lynda's murder? Is Lisa under suspicion for playing a role in murdering Lynda? That can't be! Neither is impossible! What the hell is happening?'

CHAPTER 11

Inside Interview Room No. 3, Burns and Lisa sit opposite each other. She hasn't come down from feeling betrayed by her husband. Her prior defiant behavior is still evident at this time. "Are you accusing me of something? You read me my rights but what is it I'm supposed to have done?"

"We can make this real easy for both of us. Just try to calm down. Would you like a soft drink or coffee?"

"Screw you! Charge me with something or I'm out of here."

Burns lets out a breath of air. He knows that it's only her husband's word against hers, but he pushes for a little more. "OK, here's the situation. Your husband said you confessed to him of killing Lynda Ackerman. That's what he said. That's why you're here right now. Did you or didn't you?"

She is armed with more fire power in her personality arsenal. "Oh, the man who was sleeping with her behind my back … betrayed not only his wife but his five year old daughter? Is that it? Is that all you have? Is that someone you take for being honest?"

Burns knows all too well he's on shaky ground, but for the time being, that's all he's got. "A simple yes or no will suffice."

"Alright, then it's a simple no." She crosses her arms. "Maybe he's the one you need to investigate further, like what he did with his Company, or should I say with his former Company … he just got axed and the prima donna Whitney the bitch is now in charge. Let me tell you, you'll find him, Whitehead, and Rose so corrupt you'll want to puke. I'd follow that trail than try to pin her murder on me. I've done nothing wrong." She decides now is the time to play a sympathy card, so she forces an authentic appearing cry with tears and sobbing so well-choreographed you'd vote her an Oscar without hesitation.

Burns continues to stare at Lisa. He doesn't for one minute think she killed Lynda Ackerman. For one, Lisa is not a formidable looking person in size, shape, or strength … yet maybe only demeanor. She'd have to have had somehow to lure Lynda out of her apartment, someplace very close to the dumpster in order to accomplish the act. There'd be no way she could have killed Lynda inside her apartment and then carried the body by herself, and with no one seeing her, unless, of course, there was an accomplice who did the heavy lifting. So, either Lisa had help in the murder or someone else did it. Burns' best bet is that the killer is still loose and it isn't Lisa. He knows by instinct someone knows or saw something they're not telling.

Fred wonders if in fact he is going insane, hallucinating if she is really up to it. That might explain many things simply, or it may explain absolutely nothing. However, while no tangible evidence to prove it, he still believes something for sure … he is being betrayed and it's his wife who's doing it. Fred can think of only one person to contact … one place to go … someone he hopes will believe he's still a friend.

"She's with Detective Burns now." Fred feels his heartbeat pick up.

Rose listens carefully to what Fred says, and confirms to himself it was a good idea not to contact Whitney for the unplanned out-of-office meet-up with him. He sounded desperate and spooked on the phone. Better to take it one-on-one. He asks, "What do you think she's saying?"

"Hmm, your guess is as good as mine."

Rose quickly replies, "Take a guess. She's your wife."

Fred clears his throat. "She'll deny ever confessing to me she killed Ackerman."

"Is there any evidence?"

"No, it's her word against mine."

"And you understand the legal principle of innocent unless proven guilty?"

Fred begins to show a wee bit of anger, "Of course."

"Then why the hell did you call Burns!"

Fred keeps quiet as he processes the obvious conclusion.

Rose emphasizes, "That was stupid."

"Don't remind me."

"And what is it that you want me to do?"

"Listen Hank, we go back a few years. You know … you, Charles and me. We've been through a lot together. And …."

Rose interrupts, "Cut the bullshit. Answer my question. What do you want me to do?"

"I don't believe I'm going to say this."

"Then don't say it, or else say it. What do you want from me?"

"I want Lisa to disappear … forever."

Rose doesn't shed his personality. He remains totally under control. "Do you know what you're asking?"

"Yes."

"Why?"

"She knows a lot about us … Charles, you and me. She's been able to piece the puzzle over the years." He leans towards Hank and whispers, "Hank, she knows more than she should. She's dangerous."

Rose's forehead shows wrinkles like never before. He appears worried.

Fred continues, "We could be put away for the rest of our lives. Something I'm not drawn to, nor do I suspect are you."

There is a slice of silence as Fred hears Rose breathing through his nose. The short wait is excruciating.

Then Rose asks, "Do you care how it's done and by who?"

"Be serious. We both want it professionally done, and done soon."

"Let me think about this."

Fred feels more anxious than just a short time ago. "We don't have much time."

"If we go through with this, you'll never see or hear from her again."

Fred grins although his nerves are as tight as the E-string on a guitar, the thinnest and first string. "I could be so lucky."

"And you can live with that?"

"I feel differently already just thinking about it."

"And what is the feeling?"

He exhales noisily, "Relief."

"And you might have to disappear for good yourself ... going off the grid, living another life or lives ... moving from place to place ... is vanishing yourself an option?"

"As I said, I feel relieved already."

Later the same day Rose stops by Whitney's office whose head is at an angle toward her desktop reading through what seems to be hundreds of pages of documents. She senses someone nearby so she straightens up to see Rose standing at the doorway. She smiles, "You saved me. Come on in. My head is spinning from reading all of this." She waves her right hand across the papers.

"There's something you've got to see." His voice is toned-down.

"Oh, what is it?"

"Over the years Charles and I, with little help from Fred I might add, have developed some pretty good relationships with certain people. I'll leave it at that. Detective Burns will be bringing in Jesse Sanchez for a few questions and I think you'll want to overhear it."

Whitney's eyes widen at the mention of Jesse's name.

"You do know him ... don't you."

She clears her voice before answering in order to calculate her response, but the hesitation gives Rose just enough time to provide advice.

"Now is not the time to deny. If you're ever called in for questioning of any sorts, don't perjure yourself by telling untruths."

"Yes, I do know him." She clears her throat again.

"What's your relationship with him?"

"I'd call it a friendship, nothing more, just a friendship."

"OK, then stick to that story whatever he might say." He stares for a short time without saying anything.

She smells something in the air, something unpleasant, yet she too keeps silent for a short time before saying, "But you know who he is."

"Even if I did, I wouldn't tell you. There are somethings that must stay hidden for the time being, to protect you. That's how Charles wanted it to be, and I'm going to do my best to honor his wish."

Whitney stands. "Well, show me what you've got."

"We're going to watch Burns interview Sanchez. This is a rare and restricted access that few people have, so this must be kept confidential."

"You've got my word."

The drive to the Precinct is eerily silent, neither Rose nor Whitney wanting to start up a conversation.

Standing behind a one-way mirror, Rose and Whitney watch and listen-in on Jesse and Burns. There is a small table separating the two men. Each sits in a chair.

Burns starts it off. "Tell me your full name."

"Jesse Sanchez."

"And what do you do for a living?"

"I'm a full time student working on my M. B. A.."

"Is that it, full time M. B. A. student? Or is there something else you do?"

Jesse knows that Burns knows the answer, so he figures it would be insane to deny the truth. "I'm an escort."

Burns starts to put on an act. He leans forward, hoping he's not hamming it up too much. "An escort, is that what you said? You're an escort?"

Jesse keeps his composure. "Yes sir, that's what I said."

Burns leans back in his chair, continuing the play-acting. "And specifically what does that entail?" He lays both hands flat on the table.

"Mostly whatever the client wants." His poise continues as if the answer doesn't mean much.

"Give me an example?" Burns keeps both hands flat on the table.

"It's sort of like a blind date. Usually, their original date cancelled for some reason, and they simply need someone to be with at that point in time."

Burns crosses his arms, "For example."

Jesse cocks his head to the side. "For example, they've been invited to a formal dinner and don't want to show up alone." He looks at Burns who seems not to be buying the whole idea. "Or, it could be the opening of the opera season, or the first showing of a blockbuster movie, or it might be a fundraiser. You know … those kinds of things."

"And I imagine you get paid for doing this."

"Definitely, college tuition with books is expensive. I've got to find a way to pay the bills."

"And there's nothing else you do for the payment?"

"I don't get paid by the client. I get paid through an agency at an hourly rate of $50 that after taxes is about $37.50."

"That's not what I asked." Burns leans once again

towards Jesse, replacing both hands flat on the table that separates them.

"Then, with all due respect, Detective Burns, I don't understand the question."

Burns pinches his lips tightly together, and then raises his voice. "Do you get paid for having sex with your clients?"

Jesse frowns. It's now his turn to play act. "Oh, no, that's not what this is about." He intently looks at Burns and then continues. "That would be against the law."

"And, of course, you don't want to ever break the law." His look is more sarcastic appearing than a simple stare.

"Yes sir, I don't want to break the law."

Burns smacks his lips. "Let's move on to Whitney Danica." He pauses to check out any reaction from Jesse at the mention of her name. He sees little behavioral response from him, so he continues. "Do you know Whitney Danica?"

"Oh, yes, I do." He smiles.

"You seemed pleased."

"Yes, I am."

"How do you know Whitney Danica ... how you met and what relationship you have with her?"

"Sure." Jesse clears his throat. "I was doing some research at the public library ... you know the one on Dove Lane ... one afternoon, and she was there. I'm not sure what she was doing ... maybe checking out a book or returning one, or some other business. Anyway, we struck up a conversation."

"Just like that ... struck up a conversation in the library." Burns doesn't try to hold back the sarcasm.

"Yeah, just like that." Jesse keeps a neutral looking face.

"What did you talk about?"

"Honestly, a few things here and there."

"You don't remember anything specific?"

Jesse keeps quiet as he cocks his head to the side.

Burns is insistent, so he asks again, "What do you remember ... anything?"

Jesse smiles brightly, "Oh, yeah." His eyes light up.

"Please, don't keep me waiting."

"Well, what I remember is that we started to talk about school, you know my M. B. A.. She asked me if I had a major and I said Organizational Behavior."

"Huh?" Burns isn't sure what that means, but he's not interested in knowing anything more about it, so he keeps quiet.

Jesse's smile gets brighter as he thinks about his next thought, "Then she asked me if I knew of the Fibonacci sequence." He purposely hesitates to keep Burns' attention.

Burns frowns, "The what?"

"The Fibonacci sequence is a set of numbers that starts with a zero or a one, followed by a one, and goes on based on the rule that each number, called a Fibonacci number, is equal to the sum of the previous two numbers. Here's the example. Take the series of numbers 0, 1, 1, 2, 3, 5, 8, 13, 21, 34, for example. The next number is found by adding up the two numbers before it. For example 0 plus 1 equals 1, 1 plus 1 equals 2, 1 plus 2 equals 3, and so on." He continues to smile with the same enjoyment Whitney had when she told him.

Burns cocks his head sideways and frowns, "Fine, what else?"

"I don't know what else there is?"

"Let me help you out." Burns turns his nose upward. "Have you two ever had sex?"

Jesse has been waiting for this question. Without hesitation his answer is one word, "No."

Burns cocks his head to the side again, "Never?"

"Correct."

"She isn't attractive to you?"

"Oh, no, I didn't say that, nor do I mean it. She is very and I do mean very attractive, but no, we've never had sex."

Burns isn't convinced but has no evidence. "What else have the two of you done together?"

"Ah, we've had coffee together at the café just outside the Library a few times."

"Has she told you anything about her personal life … you know, stuff that is only shared between two really close people?"

"You think we're really close to each other?"

"Aren't you?"

"I don't think so, maybe she does."

"Would you … you know what I mean." He purposely does not finish his thought as he slightly tilts his head backward. He knows his message was sent and received clearly.

Jesse smiles again, "Yes, that would be nice, but I don't think that's in the cards."

"And how do you know?"

"Detective, I don't know for sure much about anything. It's just my gut feeling."

"But you do have feelings for her."

"She's unforgettable."

Rose turns to look at Whitney whose eyes are watered. She quietly mouths something to herself that only she can hear, "He's not a confidential informant."

Rose knows the truth is always in the eyes ... the pathway to the soul, and now he knows her truth.

Back in his office, Burns rubs his forehead with the thumbs of both hands. He feels he's no closer to finding the murderer of Lynda Ackerman.

He stares at the wall clock in his office, almost eleven in the morning. He's been up since six working, first here in his office, then interviewing Jesse, and now back inside his messy office. He's had at least one full pot of the most dreadful coffee ever tasted by mankind, government-issued, that is eating away the insides of his stomach. He belches and then farts. He feels a little better.

He speaks to himself out loud the words he's already written on a white board inside his office. "Random acts, crimes of passion, arguments gone wrong, self-defense." He takes another sip of the dreadful brew and then continues as if he is carrying on a conversation with the white board. "Do I start looking for new evidence in places that are unconventional? There are only a few things I know for certain, but none are helping me solve it. What am I missing?" He continues to stare at the whiteboard as if he's waiting for a definitive answer. "Something is out of sync here." The whiteboard is silent.

Stacked in the corner of his already jam-packed office he stares at several boxes that he brought up from the Evidence Room that were taken from Lynda's apartment. He's already gone through them once before without anything jumping out at him, maybe the second time is the charm. Also, he's on a short leash with the Chief in keeping the boxes in his office when they legally should be held safely in the Evidence Room. He gets out of his chair to walk towards the corner and then reaches over to arbitrarily take hold of one box. Still standing he opens it to recheck its contents. He leafs through several items until he stops at a manila folder labeled 'photos.' For some reason he doesn't remember seeing the item the first time, but quickly shoves aside any further self-questioning of his prior action. He opens the folder to find a few photos of people's faces … some with only one person while others with two people. He frowns as he slowly examines each photo image to notice that the pictures of solo people are either a male or female about the same age as Lynda, and a few photos where Lynda and one male as well as Lynda with one female are together. There are different females and different males among the group. He wonders what it all means, but since this is his newest lead, if you can call it a lead, he's got to find the people in these photos. He makes the assumption that Lynda was into photography, so he might check out where the artsy crowd hangs out, wherever that may be.

Burns strikes out from the first two spots he visits … maybe the third one is the charm. Bingo, he shows a few sample photos to the owner of *The Coffee Roaster*, Lilli Davis, who recognizes one of the men from the photos and Lynda by appearance only … no name, address, and so forth. Lilli tells Burns that she's seen the young man and Lynda together at *The Coffee Roaster* on several occasions.

Lilli says, "From what I can remember, I've seen these

two together drinking coffee, just talking, usually in that corner." She points to a specific location within the place.

Burns asks, "Did they arrive together?"

Lilli taps her chin with the index finger of her right hand, "No, I don't think so, but I really can't be certain."

"What about leaving together? Did you see that?"

She keeps her index finger on her chin, "Can't be sure."

"Any idea as to what they were talking about?"

"Definitely I have no idea."

"What about their relationship?"

"Like, do you mean friendly or real friendly?"

"However you can describe it."

"I'd say, just friendly."

"So, no touching, hand holding, kissing, you know what I'm talking about."

"Right … none of that, at least none that I saw."

"When was the last time you saw them together?"

"Could be a few weeks ago." Lilli pauses, and then continues, "But come to think of it, he came in by himself just a few days ago and sat in the same place. As I just said, he was alone."

"Do people who come here sleep around with each other?"

Lilli looks at Burns is as if she's seen a ghost, render speechless for a short time. "What?"

"I'm just wondering who these people really are." Burns shrugs his shoulders.

"Are you accusing me of running a pick-up place?"

Burns is not dumbfounded by her reaction. "Of course not, but I had to ask it."

"Well, it wasn't welcomed." She glares.

Suddenly Lilli turns away towards a customer walking in, headed towards the counter to place his order. "That's him. Maybe you should ask him." She tilts her head upward.

Burns visually checks him out to verify he's the one, waits for him to complete the order and take a seat, not surprisingly the same place Lilli mentioned earlier.

"Excuse me." Burns flashes his badge for the man to clearly see. "Can I join you for a conversation?"

The man's eyes widen. He's taken by surprise. "Yes, of course, please." His voice, while polite, seems shaken.

Burns pulls out the empty chair to take a seat. "I'm Detective Burns, investigating a murder. I'm led to believe you know the victim. What's your name?" He pulls out a face shot of Lynda Ackerman and him together.

"My God, she's dead?" His surprise blush at first seems real enough and sincere.

"What's your name?"

"Lee Way."

"OK, Lee, so you didn't know?"

"No."

"But you were seeing her on a regular basis at this place."

"Yes, but sometimes there were days, even weeks, when we didn't talk. More due to her schedule than mine."

"And what specifically do you do?"

"I'm a student at Tanager College of the Arts majoring in Theater."

"Hmm, I see." Burns holds back a cynical comment about the value of the degree. "When's the last time you saw Lynda Ackerman?" 'Keep it personal,' Burns says to himself.

"A week … maybe more, I've been involved in this school project that sometimes I wonder how time flies by."

"What was your relationship with Lynda?"

"Friends … just friends."

"Nothing more?"

"No."

"Nothing like an artist and her subject?"

"What are you talking about?"

"Hear me out for a second." Burns waits to get at least a nod from Lee to continue.

"Sure."

"Lynda Ackerman was into photography. She had lots of photos of people she took pictures of, including you. Everyone looks real happy in the photos … I mean very happy. But, and listen to this, maybe something got out of hand between friends because one of the two wanted it to be more than friends. Get my drift?"

"Crime of passion, is that what you're saying?"

"I couldn't have said it better."

"I guess it might, but I wouldn't know."

"So you said, you were just friends with Lynda Ackerman, nothing more."

"Yes, in a manner of speaking."

"And what manner was that?"

"Not what you're thinking."

"Help me understand." Burns figures he's moving the conversation along quite well.

Lee begins to feel a little discomfort as to the way the conversation is going. "I mean I wasn't the kind of friend in ways like most of her other friends."

"And what does that mean?" Burns feels very good about the talk.

"She slept around a lot … I mean a lot … with men and with women."

"But not you … is that what you're saying?"

"Yes, not me."

"Your decision or hers?"

"Mine."

"Really?"

"Yeah, really." Lee begins to feel more comfortable and confident with his answers.

"Tell me more."

"I was more of a big brother to her."

"No shit."

"Oh, it's the truth."

"Did you have anything to do with Lynda Ackerman's murder?"

"No."

"But someone did. Someone murdered her and then dumped her body into a trash dumpster as if he, she or they were throwing away garbage. Somebody did, and you're saying you didn't."

"Correct. She was more like a sister that I never had, and probably I was more like a brother she never had."

"You're hiding something." Burns' stare locks onto Lee's.

"And what's that? What are you thinking?"

"That who killed Lynda is still around. Maybe not here, close by, but still around, and you know something."

"I don't know anything more than what I've already told you."

"How could anyone live with that … you know … killing another human being."

Lee takes in a deep breath to settle his nerves. He figures to take some advice from his acting coach to be the character. "I'm no longer surprised how easily people lie to themselves … in a way self-betrayal."

"Did Lynda belong to a photography club? You know the type I'm talking about."

"Don't know for sure, but she was one hell of a photographer. She might have been, but come to think of it, probably not."

"Why?"

"Loner, she was to the core a loner … liked being with her camera more than anyone person for any length of time. I guess she trusted her camera more than she trusted people."

"But you said she slept around?"

"Yeah, I did."

"That doesn't seem to be what a loner would do."

"Unless, of course, if sleeping around was all impersonal, nothing more."

Burns leans back in his chair, ambivalent if Lee had nothing to do with the murder of Lynda Ackerman. He wonders if he should show Lee any of the other photos to find out if he recognizes anyone else, but quickly puts that aside for the time. He takes a card out of his pocket and places it between them on the table. "If you remember something give me a call. Thanks for your time." He waits for Lee for respond.

"Sure."

Burns leaves Lee alone, yet wondering about his

involvement in the Ackerman murder. Something just doesn't fit together.

Burns returns to his office wondering if there is other information within the evidence boxes that might help. He sure could use something to provide a clue or two about Lynda's killer or killers. He'd settle for anything at this point as he reaches to open another box. Pow ... the proverbial needle in the haystack hits him squarely in the head! It is a metal box the size of a cardboard shoe box that had been previously examined but was empty. He reaches inside the evidence box for it, tosses it between his hands a few times, and then puts it on his desk. He opens the lid to find it empty, as predicted. Then he examines it further by carefully running the tips of his fingers along the inside base of the metal box. He feels something unusual so he further inspects the insides with a small but powerful flashlight to notice a loosened seal.

He pries it open to reveal a fake bottom containing several small snapshots inside a waterproof bag, along with almost a quarter-inch thick of one hundred dollar bills neatly pressed together. He takes out one of pages of small snapshots to hold up towards the ceiling lights. The images are clearly visible, specifically of Lynda and another woman in provocative seductive poses. He removes another page to inspect. This time it is Lynda with a man in sexually suggestive embraces. He goes for a third page with the same tantalizing poses of almost nakedness, but this time he recognizes Lisa Saunders. A fourth page contains Lynda and Fred Saunders in poses that leaves little left to the imagination. "My God, what was going on?" He's seen many strange things during his law enforcement career but this might be the weirdest. He takes in a deep breath of air to think though a few things. 'Did Lynda take these photos without the others' knowledge; did someone else who is not seen in the photos take the pictures; why would Lynda keep the photos hidden in a fake bottom of a metal container; what's the relevance of the money?'

He feels the need for something stronger than the crappy coffee that's been waiting for him, but he knows better than to drink on the job inside his office. He pours another cup of the dreadful liquid into a cup, and swallows it quickly thinking the obnoxious taste will be minimally felt. He's wide off the mark.

He returns to thinking about the snapshots and money. 'What was her motive to keep these? It's possible but inconceivable that she was unaware of any of this. And then there's the money.'

He reaches to grab a few of the Franklin bills to check serial numbers. 'If they're sequenced, there's a high probability drugs were involved.' But no, the numbers are not sequential.

Burns decides to make a call to Special Agent Scott Marin.

"It's about the Ackerman murder. Can you run some snapshots through your database? I might be onto a real lead?"

"No problem. Give me the names."

"There's really only one I think might be valuable. Lee

Way. He's a male, five eleven, one seventy, Caucasian light skin, brown eyes and hair, no facial scars, articulate and seems self-confident. He said he knew Ackerman in a non-intimate way, actually he said as her older brother, if you believe that." Burns chuckles.

"We've both heard that before."

"I've scanned his photo. The others I can scan later. You might have received the photo by now."

"Hmm, yeah, I just received it. If you want to hang on this shouldn't take long."

"Perfect. Must be nice to have high tech at your fingertips."

"Thanks to the taxpayers."

Burns adds an idle thought, "Anything interesting at your end that you're working on?"

"After a while, it comes down to just working on something."

"I know the feeling." Burns pauses, "Anything yet?"

"Almost done." Marin pauses, "Holy crap."

Burns feels his heart pick up. "What?"

"It seems your guy, Lee Way, has had some run-ins with law enforcement over the past few years crossing from State to State. His profile is simply this … he's acted as a part-time freelance photographer for a few small city police departments in the states of Maine, Delaware, and Maryland mainly working crime scenes."

Burns interrupts, "So he's a legit photographer."

"Definitely, but something else."

"Like what?"

"He's a con artist who's been arrested for taking illegal photos of women acting as a paid photographer from fashion magazines in search of female models. Once he shows them their partially clothed mostly nude photos he threatens to expose them unless he gets paid in exchange for the photos. He's also pretended to be a cop willing to forgive them in exchange for his victims to give him what he wants."

"He's scum."

"Among other things, but up until now, he's been off our radar, disappeared."

"Do you think he could have been involved with Ackerman's murder?"

Marin shrugs his shoulders, "Could be. Have you turned up any illicit photos of anyone connected to the case?"

"As a matter of fact, I have, and you won't believe it."

"Try me."

"Fred Saunders, his wife Lisa, and Ackerman herself. There are others, but these are the main ones."

"Holy shit, you've got quite a case. Do you think you've scared Lee to vanish?"

"Yeah, the thought has crossed my mind. We might never find Lee again, but I'm definitely going to make another visit with Fred and Lisa."

"Gonna show them their own photos?"

"Of course, alone at first and then if they give me a hard time, I'll bring them together for the entire showing." He chuckles.

"I'd like to see that myself." He laughs.

"I'll see what I can do, but no promises."

"I understand. Anything else you find when you came across the photos?"

"About a half-inch stack of Franklins without serial number sequence."

"You know what that means."

"Yeah, we can take away drug money for the time being."

"And include a hell of a lot more, like blackmail for starters."

"That's how I see it."

Fred Saunders nervously sits across from Burns. A table is the only thing that separates them in Interview Room 2.

Burns starts it off. "I appreciate you coming down to see me. I think I've got something you'd like to see."

"Sure … sure … if it helps you find the real killer."

"I think we're getting close, but, and you may not appreciate it, these cases seem to have a mind of their own at times. The key is to keep up to date. Know what I mean?"

Saunders isn't sure what Burns means but there's no sense in contradicting him now. "I guess."

"Anyway, I've got a few things I'd like you to take a look at and tell me what you think. OK?"

"Like I said, anything that helps." He blinks his eyes several times in rapid succession.

Slowly, Burns opens a manila folder in front of him. Then, one by one, he slowly slides face up one at a time five photos of Saunders and Ackerman mostly nude, with big smiles. "Recognize anyone?"

Saunders' jaw almost entirely drops off his face. Shaken up doesn't fully describe how he feels, not even close, more like traumatized. He is speechless.

"Take your time." Burns remains still, eyes glued to Saunders.

"Where … where did you get these?" It's clear that Saunders is outraged, offended, and shocked.

"Give me your best guess."

"How … how did you get these? These were supposed to have been destroyed. I paid her to destroy them." Saunders is able to now change his stare from the soft-porn photos to Burns. "Five thousand dollars cash in hundred dollar bills."

"I guess she didn't keep her end of the deal."

"What are you going to do with these?"

"They're evidence, so they remain the property of the police in the Lynda Ackerman murder."

Saunders seems to be fantasizing as he rambles on in a soft spoken manner. "Lynda was special. She had a spell on me every time we were together. I couldn't break lose."

"Did you kill Lynda Ackerman?"

The question seems to shake-up Saunders. "For God sake, no, I would never harm her … never … never."

"Well somebody did. Has your memory been sparked?"

"I don't know who would do this, but I've already told you about Lisa's, my wife's, confession to me."

"Oh, I almost forgot. She said … he said." Burns is unable to hold back some sarcasm.

"Am I a suspect?"

"No, only a person of interest, but just the same don't leave town."

Later the day, with only two hours separating the interviews to ensure the husband and wife have no opportunity to talk with one another, Lisa Saunders uneasily sits across from Burns in the same Interview Room, Number 2, with the same table the only thing separating them.

Once again, Burns starts it off. "Thanks for coming down to see me on such quick notice. I might have something you'd like to see."

Lisa remains quiet, lips tightly clenched and jaw forced downward. She hears her own breathing through her nostrils.

Burns takes one photo at a time out of the same manila folder, face down, and places them directly between her and him.

Lisa's eyes carefully follow his hand movements.

Then, one by one, he turns each photo over all the while watching Lisa's face.

At the revelation of the nature of the first photo, Lisa takes in a gasp of air. "My God!" Her voice is loud and chilling. She is worried as the remaining photos are displayed. "Oh, my God." This time her voice is barely heard.

"I'd like your comments." Burns feels in control now that the cover up is exposed.

"I ... I ... don't know what to say." She turns her head away from the photos. "Take them away. I don't want to see them."

"I'm sorry, Mrs. Saunders, but this is police evidence that is crucial to finding Lynda's Ackerman's murderer."

Tears form at the corners of both eyes, and then she begins to cry, softy at first at a mere whisper and then into a scream of fright.

Burns sits back in his chair, not necessarily enjoying seeing her pain, but realizing that soon she'll be able to talk without the bawling. He patiently waits until she stops weeping. "Talk to me." His voice is unusually reassuring. "What is this all about?"

Lisa sniffles one last time, straightens up in the chair and takes in and out needed air. She swallows. "Lynda had a way with me, and I suspect many people who got to know her. For me, I felt young and desirable, something that after I married vanished quickly. I don't know how to explain it, but that's what happened."

"I see." Burns stays connected with Lisa. "What else?"

"She was a lovely woman, very attractive and at times almost like a girl without any inhibitions … pure and simple." Lisa smiles in a lovingly way as she looks directly into the eyes of Burns, "Strange, isn't it how I just described her. Yes, I think I used some words that even surprised me."

"Were you jealous of her in any way?"

"Oh, no, not jealous, perhaps wanting to be like her, but no, not resentful, spiteful or anything like that."

"You told your husband that you killed her."

She breathes out a big breath of air. "He also was mesmerized by her. I know they slept together."

"Back to what you told him, did you?"

"Of course not, I had no motive to kill the one who made me feel wonderful."

"There were hundred dollar bills found with these pictures. I think the money was blackmail money."

"Sorry to disappoint you, Detective, but they're not from me."

"Then why did you tell your husband you killed her? That doesn't make sense."

"I agree it doesn't make sense. That's because I never said

it." She knows the last part is the truth but figures explaining the hatred she felt and still feels for her husband wouldn't make any sense to the Detective.

"Is there anything else you want to tell me at this time?"

"No Detective, there isn't. Is there anything else you want to ask me at this time?" She feels suddenly embolden.

Burns picks up on her change of attitude, but decides to let it slide. There's no value in getting into a peeing match. "Not at this time, but don't leave the City."

"Am I a suspect?"

"No, but I consider you a person of interest."

Lee thinks he's gotten away with another crime, this time a more serious one ... a murder, although unintentional.

She just didn't get it ... a promise is a promise ... you do what you say you're going to do ... it's that simple. He chose Lynda carefully ... she fit into the profile of someone who needed a strong bond with others due to her own insecurities. He convinced her that in order for her to feel good about herself, she needed to seek out others ... to get them to be attached to her ... you don't ask, you don't get. She needed to use her own qualities as well, in this case her physical beauty and seductive tendencies.

He thought he had convinced her that acting as a team ... him and her ... they could not only feel loved by others but also make a ton of money doing it. But under no conditions should she give in to love.

He taught her how to choose her targets carefully, those with deep insecurities. Pose as provocatively as needed and then get them to join in ... how simple would that be. And he would take care of the financials. And … it worked … but not long enough. He's now on the run.

He's also pissed off at Lynda who somehow hid most of the money from him. The student outwitted the teacher! He pounds the steering wheel with his right fist. "Damn her!"

He's self-assured that he'll figure out another scam because there are unlimited dupes around. Hell, he's already faked himself as a cop and a professional photographer, just to name two. He smiles as he thinks of what's next.

He continues to drive, intending to cross the State line before nightfall, find an inconspicuous motel for a few days to scheme up his next plan. Keeping his left hand on the steering wheel, he leans right to reach for a pint of Tennessee Whiskey that has already been opened. The bottle is adjacent to him on the front passenger seat.

For a deadly split second he takes his eyes off the front window to grab the Whiskey which in turn causes his left hand to jerk the steering wheel to the left. That stupid act might have prevented him from colliding head on with an oncoming truck that killed him instantly. But there's no argument now … he dies quickly.

His death is a minor footnote in the obituaries the next day.

Chapter 12

There comes a point in many professionals' lives when they ask, 'Is that all there is to my life?' which usually is the signal to think about hanging up the cleats. It doesn't matter if the professional is an athlete whose body doesn't fully recover as quickly as it used to from an injury; or the actor who's not getting calls from her agent for movie parts because she no longer fits into the studio's wheelhouse (whatever that means); or the teacher who begins forgetting her lectures that she's perfected to do a million times before (maybe it's a hundred thousand, but let's not quibble about the number); or the businessperson who's just worn out and tired of making deal after deal after deal wondering why it gets tougher and tougher and tougher to accomplish. The point is this ... there comes a time to make a life changing decision that may not be easy or even pleasurable, but that must be made regardless of the consequence ... intentional or unintentional.

Hank Rose sits in his office late at night. It's Friday, just about 10 pm and everyone has gone for the weekend, even Whitney. He pours what he thinks is a fourth shot of Makers' Mark Whiskey into a tumbler, and it's a double but who's counting. He thinks it's time to hang up the cleats to live the rest of his life in leisure and without worries. There's no family for him to be with. He's all alone.

Contemplating on how to announce the decision to Whitney is not easy. While he's enjoyed her professional camaraderie over the past several months since his best friend, Charles Whitehead, passed away, it just isn't the same without him, a guy he grew up with and whom he considered to be as close as a real brother. He believes Charles felt the same way about him.

He's financially well off as the Chief Legal Counsel of WRS, and if he packed it in right now his lucrative income would vanish quickly but his hidden investments would keep him financially just fine for a very long time. In other words, he doesn't have any money worries at all.

He takes another sip from the tumbler, and then holds the glass in his hand as if some sort of divine intervention will solve his dilemma. He waits but nothing happens, so he takes another sip of Whiskey yet with the same zero result.

Just about one full minute goes by without any profound thoughts. He tells himself that he'd settle for something superficial at the moment. His mind continues to be a dry well of ideas. Then without warning, something really crazy whizzes through his brain. He sets the tumbler on top of his desk and reaches for the phone. He dials a number that's been memorized for a short time in case this same idea struck him as important. He knows it's late at night, but, what the hell he's got nothing to lose. He waits for the phone connection to be made.

"Special Agent Scott Marin," he looks at the caller I.D. on the phone. "How are you this evening, Mr. Rose? What can I do for you?"

"I want to talk but only if I'm protected with immunity."

"Nothing guaranteed, but I think we might be able to work something out. When do you want to talk about this?

"I'm ready now."

Marin looks at his watch. It is 10:10 pm. "You want to drive to my office now?"

"I'm ready if you are."

It is fifteen minutes past midnight, several hours later. Marin asks Rose, "Does that do it?"

Rose looks exhausted. He should. He's just heaved everything he can remember over the past many years from out of his gut … names, dates, wrongdoings, and the effects of those law-breaking activities … everything. He nods his head positively. He feels remarkably relieved.

Marin says, "Let the record reflect that Mr. Hank Rose nodded in the affirmative. Mr. Rose, please verbally state so. I don't want the written record to be at variance with your voluntary testimony."

Rose looks at the transcriptionist who's momentarily stopped, waiting for him to say something. He grabs a half bottle of water to sip before he says, "Yes … that is correct."

"And are you also stating that you came to me voluntarily indicating you wanted to provide accurate information, which you have just done, about several unlawful activities that you and others that you've named have been a part of?"

"Yes, I am."

"Again, Mr. Rose, is there anything else you wish to state for the record at this time?"

"No … not at this time."

Marin looks at the clock on the wall. "Let the record reflect that it is now twenty minutes past midnight, Saturday morning, May 27, 2017. This ends Mr. Hank Rose's testimony for the time being. There may be more to come." He nods to the transcriptionist her assignment has ended. "Mrs. Holman, thanks for coming down here at this hour. I'm sure you had other things you could have been doing. Leave the information with me. Thank you again."

Now that Mrs. Holman has left the room, Marin and Rose remain together in the Interview Room.

"What's next?" Rose takes another sip of water.

"I'm going to lock a tracking device on your ankle so I know exactly where you are from this point on."

Rose puckers his brow in a frown.

"The alternative is to jail you … for your own sake. You pick which one you want."

Rose nods his head, "OK, I get it."

"Now I call in the legal beagles to figure out the next move as I make my rounds to Danica, O'Leary, Fred and Lisa Saunders, and Samuelson. Don't make contact with any of them. Should they try to talk with you ignore them all. Do you understand?"

"But I work with all of them except for Fred and Lisa. I've got to talk with them. And hell, they're bound to see the ankle bracelet."

"Then I suggest you come up with a reason not to work for a while. Take a vacation, call in sick. Hell, I don't know. You should've thought about that before you called me."

"For how long?" His face shows signs of distress.

"The legal process can be slow."

"I'm really screwed." His voice is one of worry.

"You've made your own bed."

The following Monday morning after Special Agent Scott Marin briefs Detective Burns about Rose's confession, he and the Detective agree they should make the next move together, so Burns makes a call to Fred Saunders at his home.

"Yes?"

"Mr. Saunders, this is Detective Burns. I'd like to talk with you about some late-breaking news. Can you come down to the Precinct today? If not, then I can come out to your home immediately. Which works best for you?"

Saunders hesitates. The unexpected phone call has shaken him up. He manages to collect his composure to ask, "What specifically is this about?"

"It's really not something we should be talking on the phone. Just let me say that it's very important to you. If I were you I'd want to hear immediately what I've got to say."

"Is this about Lynda Ackerman?"

"Like I said, it's not something that should be discussed over the phone. Do I come see you or do come to see me? Which one is it?"

"I'll be at your office within the hour. This better be important."

"Thank you for your cooperation, Mr. Saunders. And yes, it is very important."

Unshaven and dressed in jeans, an over-the-belt shirt

and wearing black colored Sketchers, Saunders drives alone in his car to talk with Burns, a nerve wracking journey that is taking too long yet at the same time will be quickly over with before he realizes it. He has no idea that Marin will also be present.

His meeting with Burns and Marin is in a regular sized Interview Room, Number 2.

"Thanks for coming down. Please take a seat." Burns points to a specific chair. "There's bottled water if you want some, as well as coffee which I suggest you deny … it'll eat your stomach away." He grins thinking it's a funny joke.

Saunders looks at Marin. "Who are you?"

"I'm Special Agent Scott Marin with the F. B. I.."

Suddenly Saunders' face turns bleach white. "Why are you here?"

"Providing some support to Detective Burns."

Saunders either doesn't understand or else decides to ignore it all together. He should be very worried. "Oh."

Marin continues. "Recently, Mr. Hank Rose asked to talk with me. You know him, don't you?" The sarcasm is not difficult to pick out.

"Of course, I used to work with him!" The anger is not difficult to pick out. "What about?" Now his voice sounds as if he's suffering with misery. He is nervous.

"Many things that included the late Charles Whitehead, you, him and many others, you know, the activities were broad and numerous, and apparently according to him, illegal."

Saunders leans over the table towards Marin. "Are you

saying he confessed to …?" He lets the sentence dangle in the air between them.

Burns joins in the conversation, "Oh yeah … big time." He keeps a neutral looking facial expression all the while.

"I don't know what you're referring to." Saunders crosses his arms and juts out his jaw in defiance.

Marin continues as Burns returns to being silent. "Are you telling me you've never been involved in illegal activities? Is that what you're alleging?"

"I want an attorney!"

"Mr. Saunders, you haven't been accused of anything specific. Why on earth would you want an attorney?"

"I know my rights."

"I'm sorry you feel that way. When or if you are accused of illegal activities your rights will be obeyed. I just thought I'd want to give you a heads up?"

"Is that all you've got to say?"

"I'm really not at liberty to share whatever Mr. Rose shared with me, nor the conditions we agreed to."

"Conditions, what conditions?"

"Again, Mr. Saunders, I can't share that information."

Saunders stands. His rate of breathing increases with each passing second. His eyes have widened. "Then I'm going to leave right now!"

"Yes, I understand."

Saunders steps away from the table, unsuccessfully tries to stare down the two men, turns towards the door and seems ready to leave the room, but he doesn't. He switches his looks between Marin and Burns. "I've got some things to talk about, but I want full immunity."

Marin looks at Burns with a grin, and then back at

Saunders with a straight face. "I'll see what I can do but no promises."

Later in the day Burns and Marin discuss Saunders' confession.

Marin asks, "I'm ready to call Mrs. Saunders with the same game plan."

"It's all about timing."

Marin says, "You probably understand what I'm about to say ... it's about resources and jurisdiction." Marin pauses thinking that Burns has something to voice but when all he hears is silence he continues. "The F. B. I. has over ten thousand special agents with more personnel than that assigned to non-enforcement duties. We investigate acts that are in violation of Federal law, and as we're doing with your case we assist State and local law enforcement Agencies and investigate State and local crimes when asked to by those Agencies. We typically focus on organized crime activities including racketeering, corruption, pornography, bank robbery, white collar crime such as embezzlement, and business fraud. We're at the front position against domestic terrorist activities. So, with that being said, there's going to come to a point in time that whether you want it or not the F. B. I. will take the lead in this case. That's just how Congress has it set up. There's nothing I or you can do about it."

It's Burns' turn to reply, "Understood."

Two hours later Lisa Saunders meets with Marin and Burns in the same Interview Room that was used to interview her husband. She appears unusually comfortable with the arrangement ... either for real or as an act.

"I want to make this very clear. I've never had anything to do with their criminal actions. I just happen to be the daughter of the big kahuna, Charles Whitehead, and married, unhappily so I might add, to Fred, a dishonest and unpleasant human being. Yes, I might have been complicit, perhaps and unknowingly, in their criminal activities, but I had no way to get them to stop. I feared for my life, for God's sake. They would easily kill me, torture me, or in some other way prevent me from talking with people like you, honorable men of the law." Lisa Saunders cries. She's practiced the fake behavior many times before, but this time she couldn't make it as an extra in a C-level horror movie.

Marin and Burns are pleased the entire interview has been transcribed as have the others. The best they can do at this moment in time is to let her go on. She's building a very good case against herself.

The next day Marin makes a call to Burns. "It's time to hand over the case to the F. B. I., we have the transcripts, all given voluntarily. They all want immunity but no promises were made in exchange for their testimonies under oath. It's all the Bureau needs." Marin pauses thinking Burns has something to say, perhaps even a plea not to give up the case. There is only silence, so Marin continues. "Thanks, I appreciate your cooperation. We've been working on Whitehead, Rose, and Saunders for much too long ... taken away resources that might better be utilized elsewhere, but it is what it is. You can only delay the inevitable just so long."

Without anything in his voice that seems to sound sad in having to turn over the case to Marin, Burns asks. "Anything else I can do?"

"I think a clean break is the best. I'll do what I can do to keep you updated, but no promises."

"Understood." Burns sounds at ease with the decision.

"After I review the transcripts one more time, I'll subpoena each of them."

"What about Danica, O'Leary, and Samuelson?"

"I think they're incidental. Danica and O'Leary were not in any decision making role when all of this was happening, and Samuelson was just a customer service rep of some sorts."

"So, you're going to ignore them for the time?"

"The sound of your voice suggests you have another idea."

"Let's assume that we put away the four bad actors … Whitehead, Rose, and both Saunders … actually only three since Whitehead is dead. What's going to happen to the business and to the employees who had nothing to do with the crimes?"

Marin asks, "What do you suggest?"

Burns is eager to offer a suggestion. "If you shut down WRS completely, you might set aside sufficient funds to pay each employee something, say three full years of salary and full benefits. I mean, they didn't have anything to do with what was going on … just doing their jobs, obeying the rules. I guess what I'm saying is that I don't want to harm them for something they didn't do. And most definitely I don't want the business to continue."

"Would you give Danica, O'Leary, and Samuelson a heads up?"

"Danica and O'Leary for sure since Danica is the C.E.O. and O'Leary is the President, but for Samuelson, no. He's just their H. R. guy, not important. But that's just my take."

"Makes sense." Marin pauses and then asks, "Ever think of joining the Bureau?"

"You mean, switch teams?" His voice sounds authentically surprised.

"We're both about catching the bad guys, just in different ways. We have a hell of a lot more resources than you."

"I take it as a compliment."

"You should. I might be able to pull a few strings."

"Hmm." Burns pauses. "Let's close down this case first, and then come back around later on."

"OK with me."

EPILOGUE

Betrayal ends with Hank Rose, Fred Saunders, and Lisa Saunders going to jail. Their pleas for immunity had limited influence.

We know from the story itself that Lee Way was killed in a head on car-truck collision. Law enforcement was never able to pinpoint Lynda Ackerman's murderer. As depressing as it is, some crimes are never solved.

WRS was shut down and each employee was given three full years of salary and full benefits, just as Detective Burns suggested to Special Agent Marin, with the exceptions of Whitney Danica and Karen O'Leary who were covered under specific employment contracts of much greater financial value.

Whitney and Jesse developed an authentic relationship. She had enough money and time on her hands to focus on what was important to her and Jesse seemed to be the right person for her. He was willing to give up his "job" to focus on finishing college and be the best partner he could be for Whitney. They committed to each other, and soon moved in together.

Karen decided to return to college to earn a degree in Master in Technology and Design. She was even featured as a speaker a few times on "She Talks" Internet streaming broadcasts. She'd like to find someone she could be with for the rest of her life, but for now she's settling on advancing her education in order to further her career.

Sheldon committed to turn his life around so he set his sights on Social Services as a new career… go figure. Further he intended to get in good physical shape, but that proved harder to accomplish than he thought. His secret talks with Carol McFadden were suspected by many but never proven by anyone.

Detective Burns decided to stay right where he was in local law enforcement in spite of repeated calls from Special Agent Scott Marin who continued working within the Bureau along with Special Agent Paula McEwen.

The End

Printed in the United States
By Bookmasters